D1071196

Books by Cliff Faulknor

THE WHITE CALF
THE WHITE PERIL

THE WHITE PERIL

THE WHITE PERIL

by Cliff Faulknor

Illustrated by Gerald Tailfeathers

BOSTON Little, Brown and Company TORONTO

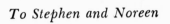
To Stephen and Noreen

ACKNOWLEDGMENTS

IN WRITING this book I am once again indebted to former buffalo ranger E. J. "Bud" Cotton of Calgary for incidents in the life of One Spot, a park buffalo he raised and finally had to kill. Details of the *Chippewa* — the first steamboat to navigate the Upper Missouri — were obtained from Michael S. Kennedy of the Historical Society of Montana, and from that fine book *Steamboating on the Upper Missouri* by William E. Lass. Many of the intimacies of Blackfoot culture came from the writings of the late James Williard Schultz. But the real flavor of that great country below "Big River" was obtained on a camping trip in those fascinating hills which ring the Judith Basin.

CLIFF FAULKNOR

CONTENTS

THE WHITE PERIL

I

◆ ◆
◆

THE INTRUDERS

Slipping his ax from his belt, Eagle Child got down on his knees and began to hack way at the ice which covered the water hole.

"Cold Maker is slow to leave us," he grumbled to his pony, Sun-in-the-Morning. "Soon it will be the New Grass Moon."

When the horse failed to snort or paw in answer, the young Piegan looked up. His heart leaped suddenly into his throat. A few yards away stood a great white buffalo bull, its nostrils steaming in the frosty morning air. Out of the corner of one eye, Eagle Child caught a glimpse of his horse — reins trailing loosely — vanishing discreetly into a grove of willows. Then his eyes widened as he recognized the intruder. He could even see traces of the scar on the bull's back which was made when his white buffalo calf had once blundered into a blazing campfire.

Without taking his eyes from the huge animal, the young Indian spoke softly: "Our little one has grown up," hoping that some familiar note in his voice would bridge the five winters that had passed since he and his father released the white calf so that it could run with its own kind.

But the wicked, watery eyes of the bull stared back at him blankly.

Eagle Child was well aware of his danger. Many were the tales told around the lodge fires of the terrible white bull that had no fear of horse or rider. He knew it was not any use to spring up and try to run for the willows. Five summers with the band's hunters had taught him that any sudden movement on his part would bring the buffalo bull charging down.

Still eyeing the beast steadily, he backed slowly away from the water hole. With a snort, the bull began to

advance toward him. Eagle Child broke out in a cold sweat. Escape was impossible.

Suddenly the beast dropped its massive head, and the young Piegan breathed a prayer to the Above Ones. He will charge now, he told himself. Then relief flooded over him, for the buffalo merely began to drink thirstily at the bubbling water hole.

Eagle Child sprang up and ran for the willows. Catching Sun-in-the-Morning, he vaulted nimbly into the saddle. He was halfway up the rise above the water hole before he reined in and looked back. Below stood the great white bull, looking after them in an odd manner as if he were puzzled about something.

"Yes, our little one remembers," Eagle Child nodded. But just the same, he was glad to be getting out of there.

Near the top of a distant rise Eagle Child stopped and carefully scanned the rolling plains around him. His father, Chief Night Rider, had taught him never to crest a hill or ridge so that he would be outlined against the sky, but to pause just below so that only his head appeared. In enemy country he would have taken even greater care, dismounting and inching forward on his stomach. But this was Piegan territory. It was this constant vigilance which had kept the Piegans and their Blackfoot cousins, the North Blackfeet and the Bloods, in their dominant position on the Western Plains.

High above Eagle Child, great V's of wild geese were winging their way to the land of Many Lights. Looking in that direction, he could see the smoke from the lodges of his people camped along Bear River. To the west, bright early-morning rays of Natos, the sun, shone on the snow-clad peaks of the mighty Backbone.

But it would be from the east or south that trouble might come. The head scout, Broken Nose, had told them this as they had ridden out just before dawn on their morning patrol. On the heights above the encampment they had parted, each moving off to the sector which had been assigned to him.

Far to the east lay their enemies the Assiniboin; closer were their friends the Gros Ventres. To the south and east was the land of the wily Crow, even worse enemies than the Assiniboin, if that were possible. But the Blackfeet had ceased to worry about their Indian neighbors. Many said the real threat lay in the white men who were rapidly gaining in strength and pushing boldly into their lands. Already they had established a great camp called Many Houses on Big River, not more than two days' ride away.

Suddenly Eagle Child's eye caught the beginnings of a dust cloud in the south. For several moments he watched it, undecided. It was advancing very slowly — too slowly for a troop of mounted warriors. Maybe it was a herd of buffalo. But it could be some of those curious rolling lodges the white man used.

"The Head Chief has said we must watch the white man whenever he passes through our land," he said to his horse. Long ago Eagle Child had formed the habit of talking things over with Sun-in-the-Morning.

The red pony snorted as in agreement.

Digging in his heels, Eagle Child urged Sun-in-the-Morning into a gallop with the "Sh, sh!" sound used by his people. He would ride on and tell Broken Nose about the dust cloud and let the Head Scout decide.

Broken Nose and the others were already waiting in the rendezvous coulee when Eagle Child arrived. With the Head Scout was another veteran, Red Quiver, and two young scouts of Eagle Child's age, Driftwillow and Slides-to-the-Ground.

"I saw a dust cloud coming from the direction of Big River," he told them. "It moved too slowly to be riders. Could it be more of the rolling lodges of the white man?"

"Did the cloud spread for many buffalo arrows?" Broken Nose asked. "Or was it a small cloud?"

Eagle Child's dark face took on a deeper hue. "I didn't wait to see," he admitted sheepishly.

Broken Nose sighed and exchanged looks with Red Quiver. The latter shrugged helplessly. These young ones are so careless, the gesture seemed to say. They are not as keen as we were at that age.

"A dust cloud can tell you many things," Broken Nose explained patiently. "A small light cloud which moves quickly says that a small band of riders approaches. A small heavy cloud could mean the rolling lodges of the white man. But a great, heavy cloud which stretches for many buffalo arrows could mean a herd of buffalo."

Eagle Child's face brightened. "It could be buffalo. This morning I saw the white bull."

"He was alone?" Broken Nose asked.

Eagle Child nodded. He told them how he had been surprised by the bull while kneeling by the water hole.

They looked at him incredulously, almost in awe.

"It is said this bull has killed many hunters," Broken Nose grunted. "Yet he let you go unharmed?"

"Perhaps he remembers how I cared for him when he was small," Eagle Child suggested.

Broken Nose shook his head in wonder. Surely the Above Ones must keep a watchful eye on this son of Night Rider's.

"If the White One is here the main herd cannot be far," Red Quiver pointed out.

"I will ride to Bear River to tell them that the buffalo have come," Slides-to-the-Ground volunteered.

"First we will ride to the dust cloud and see what it is," Broken Nose remarked pointedly.

As the wind was blowing straight from the Backbone, the Piegan scouts approached from the east. They did not want any buffalo to scent them. Below the last ridge they dismounted and crept forward. It was a buffalo herd, all right. Not a large one, but big enough to supply all the lodges in their encampment. The animals were traveling slowly, stopping to crop the wispy plains grass that had bleached white under the winter's snow.

"They are heading toward the land of the north traders," Eagle Child observed.

Broken Nose nodded. "If they are not alarmed they will pass close to our lodges."

"Now shall I ride to Bear River?" Slides-to-the-Ground asked.

"Red Quiver will ride with the news and you will

ride with him. It is said that two voices are stronger than one."

Red Quiver grinned broadly, but Slides-to-the Ground looked crestfallen. Nobody in the band appeared to take him seriously.

Just then, the ambling herd below them broke into a run. To the south, the sudden bark of guns could be heard. Mounting quickly, Broken Nose and his party galloped furiously in the direction of a sage-girt butte which would command a view of the whole basin.

"Keep low!" Broken Nose cautioned them and they scrambled up the slope. "We must not be seen."

Driftwillow pointed excitedly from the top. "They are white men. I can see some of the rolling lodges beyond them."

Behind the herd they could make out several riders moving swiftly. There were sudden puffs of smoke, each followed by the sound of a shot.

"White hunters," Broken Nose said bitterly. "If we do not stop them there will be no meat for our bellies and no robes for our backs."

"We are only five," Red Quiver reminded him. "There is only your gun."

This was quite true. Broken Nose's muzzle-loader was the only gun they had. The rest were armed with bows, axes and hunting knives.

Eagle Child, who had been closely watching the scene below, added some even more sobering information. "They have the new guns like the one my father captured many summers ago. See, they do not have to stop to reload."

Soon the dust clouds kicked up by the hooves of the alarmed herd obscured the alien riders. The dust began to spread in all directions as the frightened animals sought to put as much distance as possible between themselves and the menace behind them.

"Because of these white men there will be no fresh meat in our lodges this day," Red Quiver growled.

Broken Nose nodded angrily. "We must send word to Night Rider so that he can tell the Head Chief of these intruders."

"Chief Many Buffalo is getting old," Driftwillow snorted. "He will do nothing."

"Many Buffalo is a great warrior," Eagle Child protested. "Do you forget so soon how he saved us from the

Assiniboin? The Head Chief has said we can do nothing since all the Blackfoot chiefs signed the treaty at
Yellow River."

"Treaties!" Red Quiver scoffed. "They make
treaties only to gain time until they are stronger."

Eagle Child was inclined to agree with this. In fact,
he had heard his father, Chief Night Rider, say this
many times. But he did not like to hear Many Buffalo
derided.

"We have wasted enough time talking," Broken
Nose growled. "Let us move closer so we can see how
many guns they carry."

"All white men have guns," Red Quiver said gloomily.

From behind a low ridge five pairs of dark eyes
scanned the newcomers. On the plains below, a dozen
white men were busily skinning and butchering some
slaughtered buffalo.

Driftwillow laughed scornfully. "They are clumsy
and slow. See, one of them has dropped his knife."

"I count only four of the rolling lodges," Eagle
Child said. "But there are many horses. Do you think it
is a war party?"

Broken Nose shook his head. The big scout's eyes
gleamed avidly as he surveyed the horses.

"A trading party, seeking the skins of the beaver and
buffalo," he decided.

"Maybe they hunt the yellow rock," Red Quiver
suggested.

"It is possible," the Head Scout nodded.

"Why do white men prize the yellow rock?" Slides-to-the-Ground queried. "It is good for nothing."

"Wolf Calf says the yellow rock is the White Man's medicine," Eagle Child told him.

"Keep your heads down!" Broken Nose said sharply.

Driftwillow scoffed. "I have heard white men can ride all day and see little."

Red Quiver pointed. "There is one of them down there who sees much — that one who wears the skin of the deer. As he works see how his eyes roam the country around him!"

"Some people look much and see nothing," Driftwillow grunted.

"A man who dresses like an Indian may think like an Indian," Red Quiver said.

Broken Nose raised his hand, indicating that it was time to leave. Silently they slid down from the ridge and made their way back to their horses.

The Head Scout turned to Red Quiver. "You will take this one," he indicated Slides-to-the-Ground, "and ride swiftly to Bear River. Tell Night Rider that more white men have come to kill our buffalo. Tell him about the one who wears the deerskin. We will watch them as the Head Chief has ordered."

"Remember the guns that load quickly," Red Quiver cautioned his friend as he moved away.

"The strangers will never know of our presence," Broken Nose promised.

But back on top of the lookout ridge he was not so sure. When he crawled forward on his stomach and peered over, he noticed that the skin-clad one had stopped working and was sitting with his gun beside him.

Eagle Child and Driftwillow's mouths watered as they watched the strangers carrying pieces of buffalo toward their lodges. It had been a long time since they had had much fresh meat.

"They take only the buffalo humps and skins," Driftwillow observed. "Maybe they will leave and we can help ourselves."

"We will hunt our own buffalo!" Broken Nose snapped. "We are not scavengers!"

As the sun climbed higher the ground lost some of its frosty chill. They lay back and waited.

2

WHY DO YOU COME HERE?

Before the sun was directly overhead, Chief Night Rider arrived with a party of thirty warriors. Wolf Calf, the Medicine Man, was with them, and the later's apprentice, Sun Boy. Night Rider and Wolf Calf climbed up to where Eagle Child, Driftwillow and Broken Nose waited. Below them, the white men were now making camp beside their wagons.

"The quickest way to find why they have come here is to ask them," Night Rider grunted.

"It could be a quick way to join the Above Ones," the Medicine Man said dryly. "They might start shooting."

"A frightened man shoots without thinking," the Chief agreed. "First we will let them know we are here, and that we outnumber them. Then some of us will ride down and hold council."

"We do not outnumber them if they have the new guns," Wolf Calf said.

"And who among us speaks the white man's language?" Broken Nose wanted to know.

"If we talk sign, the one who wears the deerskin will

understand us," Wolf Calf told him. "His kind are wise in the ways of our people."

The Head Scout would be the best one to send down there with Night Rider, the Medicine Man decided. If things went wrong, the band could not afford to lose two leaders.

But Night Rider had other ideas. "You will take fifteen riders and circle around toward the Backbone," he said to Broken Nose. "Signal when you are ready. We will all ride into view to show them they are surrounded. Then Wolf Calf and I will ride down and talk with them.

"Let me go with you, Father!" Eagle Child cried eagerly. "I am not afraid!"

"Sometimes it is good to fear if fear lends caution," Night Rider smiled. But he agreed that Eagle Child should go down and meet the white men with him. It was necessary that his son learn to deal with these strangers, he reasoned.

From the sheltered area behind the hill the four of them watched Broken Nose ride off with half the warriors. Then they climbed down into the draw where the remainder of their men were guarding the horses.

Night Rider motioned for Red Quiver to join him. "Station yourself near the top of the ridge where you can see Broken Nose's signal," he ordered.

Some time later, a coyote yapped. Looking to the ridge, they saw that Red Quiver was waving. The whole party mounted quickly and rode up to join him. When all the riders were in position, the Chief raised his arm. As one man they crested the ridge and sat in

their saddles quietly waiting. Across the valley Broken
Nose and his party appeared at almost the same instant.
Not a sound had been uttered.

There was a sudden flurry of activity in the white
man's camp below them. Men scurried away from the
fire where they had been busy with the noonday meal.
Guns appeared everywhere. Only the tall one in buckskin stood motionless, waiting.

"We will go down now," said Night Rider. He indicated that Wolf Calf and Eagle Child would accompany him.

As they neared the camp, a fat man who stood beside
the one in buckskin suddenly raised his gun. Eagle
Child had an arrow in his bow before his father stopped
him.

Eagle Child relaxed when he saw that the tall man in
buckskin had knocked the other's gun down angrily.

"It is not good to fear when fear leads to panic,"
Night Rider told him. "The Fat One showed panic. If
he had pulled the trigger of his gun many men would
have died here, both whites and Indians."

"He would have been the first to die," growled Eagle
Child.

"When two men face each other, the one who shoots
first wins the battle," Wolk Calf observed dryly.
"When many men face each other, the battle only be-
gins. But young men do not think of this."

They stopped and waited. Chief Night Rider raised
his hand in a gesture of friendship. The Tall One responded and strode out to meet them. He spoke some

words in a strange tongue. But from its sound Night Rider knew that it was some Indian dialect.

"He speaks in the Sioux tongue," Wolf Calf grunted. "Some of this I learned when I was a young man."

"Good," Night Rider nodded. He indicated to the stranger that the Medicine Man would converse with him. Wolf Calf would learn much, he told himself. The Medicine Man was shrewd, and he had always served as the band's official spokesman.

Wolf Calf and the stranger sat down facing one another with their legs crossed in front of them, Indian fashion. Eagle Child and his father noted that the white man did this with ease, as if long accustomed to it.

"He is as tall as Broken Nose, that one," Eagle Child observed. "And he sits like one of our people."

"I think he is half Indian and half white," Night Rider said. "The blood of both races flows in his veins."

The parley going on in front of them seemed to be progressing favorably. When Wolf Calf came up against some Sioux terms he was not familiar with, the stranger expertly switched to sign language. The Medicine Man signed to him in return.

"Why do they come here?" Night Rider broke in impatiently. "They are far west of the trail the fur seekers use to travel to the land of the north traders."

"These men do not seek hides or fur," the Medicine Man told him. "They seek the yellow rock in the streams which flow down to join Big River."

The white man said a few words and gestured with one arm toward the Backbone.

"He says their route lies in to the mountains," Wolf Calf explained. "And when they kill they kill only for meat."

"Tell him when they shoot they stampede the buffalo away from our camping grounds," Night Rider instructed.

Wolf Calf spoke haltingly in Sioux and emphasized his point with a few lines traced on the ground with his knife.

The white man nodded and signed that he understood. Then he took his own knife and made lines of his own.

"What does he say?" Night Rider asked.

"He says he is sorry they stampeded the buffalo. This

will not happen again because they have all the meat they will need for their journey."

The Chief grunted sourly. "Tell him we will convey his words to our Head Chief, Many Buffalo," he said, "and that Many Buffalo commands many warriors."

As Wolf Calf climbed back onto his horse, Night Rider lifted his hand to the stranger in a parting salute. Then he beckoned to Eagle Child and the three of them rode slowly back up the hill.

"I wonder if they carry the burning water of the fur seekers?" Wolf Calf reflected.

"The burning water is a poison," Chief Night Rider growled. "It will destroy our people."

The Medicine Man nodded. "It is as you say. Many of our people trade skins for burning water when they should be trading for guns and powder. But the yellow rock seekers carry a poison too in their hearts — it is said the yellow rock drives them mad."

"The rock seekers are few," Night Rider shrugged. "Most seek skins and hides."

Wolf Calf shook his head gloomily. "If they find the yellow rock in our streams white men will pour into Blackfoot country in great numbers. We will have to fight them."

Night Rider looked thoughtful. "Perhaps what you say is true," he agreed. "We must try to learn if any of the yellow rock is found."

When they gained the top of the ridge where the others were waiting, the three emissaries turned and gazed at the white man's camp for a moment. Suddenly Night Rider raised his arm in a signal to Broken Nose on the far ridge. A moment later both ridges were vacant, except for a thin cloud of dust which soon dissolved into the clear, dry air.

Leaving two warriors behind to keep the gold seekers under constant watch, Night Rider and his party rode off in the direction of Bear River.

They had gone only a short distance when a single rider appeared, racing toward them at a gallop. Eagle Child recognized the gray pony Coyote when horse and rider were still a long way off.

"It is my brother, War Bonnet!" he cried.

When War Bonnet drew up in front of his father he brought news that caused their weather-beaten faces to break into smiles.

"Buffalo!" he cried. "Thousands of them! They are moving up from the direction of Big River. Our Head Chief is organizing a great hunt!"

3

◆ ◆
◆

A NARROW ESCAPE

EAGLE CHILD hit the center of the big buffalo herd just a few paces behind his father. Sun-in-the-Morning was almost as fast as Antelope Runner, the young Piegan noted. The older horse was beginning to show his years.

Through the swirling dust, Eagle Child saw a sleek cow pass in front of him. He swung his pony after it with a quick tug on the rawhide reins. Sun-in-the-Morning responded to a heel prod with a burst of speed, but it was some moments before the young hunter was able to move into position on the right side of his plunging quarry.

Drawing an arrow deftly from the quiver at his left shoulder, he fitted it to his bow. Then he drew back until the head almost touched his hand. He released the arrow at the big, hairy shoulder which bobbed before his eyes. The shaggy beast let out a bellow of pain as the arrow found its mark. But it kept running.

Sun-in-the-Morning swerved obediently away as his young master reached for another arrow, then moved in again for a second shot. This time, the wounded cow tumbled over in a shower of dust and lay still.

Eagle Child shouted in triumph. Killing a full-sized buffalo was still a rare enough occurrence to give him a thrill.

As he turned to seek another quarry, his friend Sun Boy flashed by on a brown pony he had obtained in a trade last fall. Eagle Child dug his heels into Sun-in-the-Morning and went charging after the other. "Now we will see which has the best hunter," he told himself with a grin. The brown was much younger than Sun-in-the-Morning, but the red pony had shown little evidence that his pace was slowing down.

All at once the dust thinned as they thundered over a dried slough where the prairie grass grew thick. Eagle Child caught a glimpse of his friend just ahead of him. Suddenly he heard the angry snort of a charging buffalo bull. Rising in his saddle, he shouted a quick warning. But his voice was lost in the thud of flying hooves.

There was a scream of pain from the brown pony at the sickening impact of a ton of angry buffalo. Horse and rider were knocked sprawling into the grass.

Eagle Child saw Sun Boy rise to one knee, then fall back again, clutching his right leg. The brown pony lay still. Blood was beginning to flow from an ugly gash in its side.

Eagle Child flung himself off Sun-in-the-Morning and reached his friend in a couple of bounds. He was helping Sun Boy up onto his pony when he heard a warning shout. Swinging around, he saw a great bull bearing down on them. As he braced for the shock, his eyes registered the fact that the charging bull was pure white!

Then a curious thing happened. When it was almost upon them, the big bull swerved, went charging off a few paces, then whirled and just stood there snorting and heaving. The great shaggy creature seemed confused, as if uncertain what his next move should be.

Eagle Child took advantage of this to jump up behind Sun Boy and move off toward a group of riders who had paused in the hunt to stare at them in amazement. War Bonnet was among those of his own band who observed the incident.

"You moved quickly, brother," he said with admiration. "It is said the white bull shows no mercy."

"He has killed many riders," a warrior nodded excitedly. They all looked at young Eagle Child with wonder.

"It is because he remembers," Eagle Child told his brother. "We must get a travois for Sun Boy. I think his leg is broken."

Sun Boy had slumped down in the saddle in front of him. Although his face was strained, not a groan of pain escaped his lips.

Wolf Calf rode up as they were easing the injured youth down onto the grass. One of the other warriors had gone to get somebody to bring a travois.

When the Medicine Man heard what had happened, he decided that the time had come to put an end to any idea that Eagle Child enjoyed special protection from the Above Ones. He preferred to have such rumors spread about Sun Boy, who was his apprentice.

"The white bull takes orders from Sun and the other Above Ones. He would not harm a young man who is learning to be a Sun Priest," he told them.

But privately he wondered if perhaps he had not made a mistake four summers ago when he chose Sun Boy to follow in his footsteps. He should have foreseen the return of the white buffalo, and realized that the beast would retain some feeling for Eagle Child and the pony Sun-in-the-Morning. They had been the bull's constant companions during its calfhood. A Sun Priest who could claim kinship with a white bull would carry great prestige in tribal councils.

"You hear that, brother?" War Bonnet said. "You risked your life without need. The white bull wouldn't have harmed Sun Boy."

Wolf Calf looked at the speaker sharply, but War Bonnet's eyes were wide with innocence. The Medicine Man did not care for this older son of Chief Night Rider's. He felt that the other did not show him the respect due a Sun Priest.

"It is good for a man to risk his life for another," he said with great dignity.

Later, they found that Sun Boy's leg was badly bruised, but not broken.

But word of Eagle Child's exploit spread quickly. Men and their womenfolk talked of it as they skinned and butchered their kills. And in their talk they re-

ferred to Eagle Child as "the white buffalo's friend."
Had not Sun chosen Eagle Child to find and save the
white one five winters past?

"Wolf Calf says the white bull takes his orders from
Sun," they nodded, "which means the High Above One
favors the son of Night Rider. Could it be that Sun has
great plans for our people?"

Eagle Child heard some of this talk and his heart
swelled with pride. If the Above Ones had singled him
out for a special favor who could stand against him? He
longed for a chance to go out with a war party so that
he could count coup on some formidable enemy. To
defeat a foe or take his gun or horse was to win a
"coup" — this was a badge of honor.

But his father was inclined to scoff at any idea that
his younger son was a favorite of the Above Ones. "The
Above Ones favor the warrior who is strong and resourceful," he said. "There is nothing strange in the fact
that an animal should remember one who has raised
it."

Wolf Calf was thankful that the Chief had taken this
attitude. Perhaps the people would heed him and soon
forget this silly talk. Only a Sun Priest should have the
ear of the Above Ones.

That night there was much joy in the camp along
Bear River. Soon it would be the Moon of New Grass
and many more buffalo herds would be moving up
from their wintering grounds. For the past two months
the bands had been subsisting on deer and antelope

shot in the river breaks. Now they would be able to go out on the plains and follow the buffalo for the spring hunting.

But for some of them there would be a change this year. It had to do with the increasing numbers of white men in Blackfoot territory.

In Night Rider's lodge, Eagle Child and War Bonnet sat quietly eating with their father and old Red Hawk. Every once in a while the young men stole a glance at Night Rider, but the Chief's face told them nothing.

The brothers knew that Night Rider would attend a meeting of all the band chiefs tomorrow in the Council lodge of Head Chief Many Buffalo, which was located a few miles below them. But they could see that their father was in one of his "think" moods, and they hesitated to break into his reveries.

As it happened, their mother Gray Dove did it for them. Scraping out dinner pots with the help of old Sounding Wind, Red Hawk's woman, she asked anxiously, "Are the chiefs talking of war against the white man?"

Night Rider shrugged. "We must consider it."

"When a fire starts in the long grass you stamp it out while it is still small, or soon it will become a giant which devours everybody," Old Red Hawk nodded.

"It is said the white man is already a giant in the lands beyond the sunrise," Gray Dove said. "And that they have many guns of the new kind."

"Much has been said," her husband grumbled, "but

little proof has been offered. We cannot decide what to do until we know the truth of these sayings."

"Rising Wolf has said this, and he is our friend," Gray Dove retorted. She was referring to a white man of the north traders who had become an adopted Piegan.

War Bonnet's young wife, Bright Star, busily sewing a new set of garments for her husband, said nothing. Until she became more used to her in-laws she preferred to remain silent. But this talk of a big war disturbed her. Many times she had heard Gray Dove speak of the band's great battle with the Assiniboin five summers ago. Wars meant the loss of loved ones.

But Eagle Child seized on his father's words eagerly. "You mean that many scouting parties will be sent to far-off places?" Eagle Child had already heard rumors of this.

"It is well that we learn the true strength of the white man," Night Rider admitted cautiously. "We have seen few here, but it is said that large numbers have moved into the Always-Summer-Land far to the south of us. Many more have been seen beyond the Backbone. It is also true our Head Chief has suggested we send out scouting parties to learn more."

"When do we go?" War Bonnet cried.

"No one can be spared until after the spring hunting," said his father, and he got up to show the conversation was at an end.

Eagle Child had never been beyond the Backbone, or south of Big River. If scouting parties were to be

sent out later, he vowed he would do his best to be in-
cluded in one of them.

Reading her younger son's thoughts as completely as
though he had voiced them, Gray Dove felt her heart
sink. She did not relish the idea of Eagle Child going
into some strange land where there would not be people of his own race to aid him if he got into trouble.

4

MANY HOUSES

Broken Nose signaled for his party to halt and rest in a grove of aspen. From the look of the country around them, the others knew they were close to Many Houses, the white man's main camp on Big River.

For five days they had tramped steadily along, leading their solitary pack horse. The weather was much warmer now and they were hot and dusty.

"We will tie our horse here and see if there is much movement around Many Houses," Broken Nose said.

Eagle Child felt a thrill of excitement. The real part of their adventure was just beginning. He was glad that a scouting party from his band had been selected to reconnoiter the land from Many Houses to Elk River. It would all be strange territory to him.

Eagle Child was also happy that his father had insisted that he go with the scouts, in spite of his mother's objections. Night Rider felt that somebody from the Chief's family should go. Much to War Bonnet's disgust, he had chosen Eagle Child.

"He is younger, and he needs the experience," Night Rider said.

Beyond the aspen grove, the rolling plains dropped sharply in a series of steep breaks leading to Big River. Following the Head Scout's lead, Eagle Child, Woodpecker, Red Quiver, Slides-to-the-Ground and Sun Boy crouched down as they approached the edge. About a mile below them (six buffalo arrows by the red man's measure) Big River took a wide sweep toward the far shore, leaving a broad bench on their side. Near one end of this, and close to the river, was a single row of about a dozen log and mud dwellings. Two larger buildings, surrounded by a high mud wall, stood near the shore. There had been much tree-cutting along the riverbank.

"There are not very many houses," said Eagle Child, disappointed. It had not grown much since he had seen it two winters ago. Why, he had seen great camps of his own people with several hundred lodges.

"There are not very many white men now," Red Quiver told him. "But the Head Chief has said that more will come. When they do, they will come by Big River to Many Houses."

"Look!" said Sun Boy. "There are some lodges, and more among the trees across Big River!"

Broken Nose lifted a hand to his eyes for the sun stood at the midpoint in the sky, and looked at the ones directly below. "I cannot make out their tipi markings, but I think they are our people!"

"They are from the band of Lone Eagle that makes winter camp near where Bear River joins Big River," Woodpecker nodded. He was said to have the sharpest eyes in Night Rider's band.

"Who are those camped across Big River?" Sun Boy wanted to know. Wolf Calf had insisted that his helper accompany the party so that he would not have to rely on Night Rider for a report of what they found. Sun Boy was the party's Sacred Pipe man whose visions would guide them through the dangers ahead.

Woodpecker shrugged. "It is too far to see. Perhaps they are Crow or Assiniboin come to trade buffalo robes or beaver for the burning water."

"Maybe they trade for guns," Driftwillow suggested.

"They wouldn't dare to camp so openly in Blackfoot country," Red Quiver scoffed. "No doubt they are the Entrails People." This was a Blackfoot nickname for the Gros Ventres.

"Are *we* going to trade for guns?" Eagle Child asked Broken Nose eagerly. He knew that the pack horse they led was loaded with robes and skins.

Night Rider had ordered the scouting party to go right into Many Houses and mingle with the people there. He had also asked that Broken Nose get what guns and ammunition he could before starting southward. Guns were the weapons of the future. They shot farther.

"We need three more guns," Broken Nose agreed.

Eagle Child, Sun Boy and Slides-to-the-Ground exchanged happy glances. This meant they were all to have guns. Only the older men had them now.

Seeing their expressions, Red Quiver was amused. "Having a gun will not make one a great warrior unless he learns how to use it."

"It is not the noise that kills," Woodpecker grinned. "The ball must hit where you aim."

"Ha!" scoffed Eagle Child. "Give me a gun and I will hit what I shoot at." He did not tell them his father had taught him to shoot three winters ago.

Broken Nose signaled for them to return to the pack horse: "We will go down and talk with Lone Eagle's people and find where we must go to trade."

There were only nine Piegan lodges in the valley below. The arrival of Broken Nose's party was met by barking dogs and shouting children. A tall Indian strode out to meet them.

Woodpecker shouted a greeting. "It is Running Bear," he told Broken Nose. "I rode with him against the Assiniboin."

"I am glad to see more of our own tribe down here," Running Bear said, after greetings were exchanged. Other men from the camp joined them.

"What is the trouble?" Broken Nose asked.

"More and more white men are coming to Many Houses. There is a steady flow of their keel boats on Big River. Some say the whites have big fire boats far to the south that do not have to be paddled — that soon these too will be bringing goods and men."

Broken Nose looked skeptical. "Many Houses doesn't seem to be growing."

"Few of them stay here. But while they are at Many Houses they cause trouble. Some have come to this camp to annoy our people."

"They must be taught a lesson," Woodpecker

growled. "If a Blackfoot can be abused in Blackfoot country our enemies will no longer respect us!"

The others nodded assent. Eagle Child felt a wave of anger that such a thing could happen. For generations his people had commanded the respect and even fear of neighboring tribes.

"Where do these newcomers go?" Broken Nose asked. "We have seen few of them on Bear River."

Running Bear pointed. "Some leave Big River at this point and go toward the Backbone. Others continue upriver. It is said that the yellow rock has been found in many places."

"Soon our Head Chief will arrive with many lodges of our people," Broken Nose consoled him. "They bring buffalo robes and skins to trade for guns, balls and powder."

"There are not many guns," Running Bear grunted. "It takes many robes or skins to get one."

Eagle Child and the other two young warriors looked disappointed.

"How many?" Broken Nose asked, pointing to their pack animal. "Do we have skins and robes enough for three guns?"

Running Bear grunted. "It would be possible, if the trader had guns to spare. Once I obtained a gun for ten beaver skins."

"Can you speak the white man's tongue?"

"Some words I speak," said Running Bear. "Mostly, I talk sign. But the white trader speaks our language as well as you do."

"Will you come with us to see this trader?"

Running Bear nodded. "I go often to see him."

Eagle Child and his friends looked around curiously as they walked through the timbered gateway of the fort. They could see that the walls were made of river clay — soaked with water and then baked hard in the sun.

In front of the larger building stood a white man, heavy of build and wearing a blue coat with buttons of shining brass. He raised his hand in friendly greeting.

"We call this white man Badger Head," said Running Bear as they approached.

Eagle Child was surprised at the man's eyes. They were sky color. But they were kind eyes. Not pale like the sky in winter, but deep blue like the summer sky over the Backbone.

"Welcome, Pikuni men," said the trader in their own language. Piegans are called "Pikunis" in the Blackfoot tongue.

"They bring you greetings from our Head Chief, Many Buffalo," Running Bear said. "Also they bring buffalo robes and beaver skins to trade."

"Good," the trader nodded. And addressing himself to Broken Nose, "How is my good friend Chief Many Buffalo?"

"He is well," Broken Nose replied. "Soon he will be here with many of our people."

"That is good," the trader said again, rubbing his hands in a gesture that puzzled Eagle Child and the others.

While Slides-to-the-Ground and Woodpecker held

the bridle of the horse, Red Quiver and the rest began to undo the pack and lay the robes and skins out on the ground. But a sharp wind blowing from the Backbone made it difficult to keep them there. In all, there were six robes and twenty beaver pelts.

"Bring them inside," the trader said, leading the way into the building.

When they had finished hauling in the skins, Eagle Child and his friends looked in awe at the wealth of goods piled around them. There were kettles and pots, knives, axes and blankets. There were bolts of brightly colored cloth and many boxes, big and small. The white man must be a worker of miracles, thought Eagle Child, to produce goods that are so fine.

"Badger Head," said Broken Nose, using the trader's Indian name. "We need three guns. Soon we must travel through land where many enemies lurk."

The man shrugged. "I have only one gun to trade. Soon a big boat will come and I shall have more."

This was a bitter disappointment, but Broken Nose had been half prepared for it, from what Running Bear had said. If he obtained one more gun it would mean his party would have a total of four.

"This gun you have — is it one that loads from the back?"

"It is only a north trader's muzzle-loader," the trader told him regretfully. "Just like the ones you have."

They finally settled for the gun, a short ax, four knives and a good supply of balls and powder. This took sixteen of the beaver skins. Not being interested in camp goods, they decided to leave the robes and remaining skins with Running Bear.

As they were going out the door, Eagle Child lingered for one last look at all the wonderful things stacked around the room. When he turned to follow his friends he collided with a burly white man who had just come in the door.

"Look where yer goin', you pesky redskin!" the newcomer roared, giving Eagle Child a violent shove. Although the move caught the young Piegan by surprise, he was able to keep his balance and stay on his feet. He did not know what the man had said to him. But the meaning of the act itself and the contempt in the man's voice were unmistakable.

Eyes blazing, Eagle Child drew his knife and sprang toward the offender. But Badger Head, the trader, was even quicker. Stepping nimbly forward, he sent the white man sprawling with a blow of his fist.

Eagle Child looked from one to the other, undecided what he should do.

"He is a stranger," the trader said quickly in Blackfoot, "one of the yellow rock seekers. He will not remain long in Many Houses."

Just then Broken Nose and the others rushed in the door. Red Quiver had his gun in his hands ready to use as a club.

The trader repeated what he had said to Eagle Child. The newcomer was an uncouth person, ignorant of the ways of Blackfoot country. All this time the stranger sat on the floor nursing his jaw and saying not a word.

Broken Nose pointed to Eagle Child. "He is our

Chief's son," he told the trader. "His father would not be happy to hear of this."

"The stranger is a nothing person — a seeker of the yellow rock — soon he will be gone," the trader assured him.

"It would be well if he does not seek the yellow rock near one of our camps," Red Quiver growled.

As they left the building they could hear the trader and the newcomer shouting at each other in angry tones.

It was not the violence of the encounter which disturbed Eagle Child, but the contempt he had heard in the stranger's tone. Hate between races he could understand. Did not he and his friends all hate the Crow? But why should this white man have contempt for him? He had never lacked courage or resourcefulness in time of danger, or refused to share what he had with a friend in time of need. Did not this newcomer see that Eagle Child belonged to the mighty Blackfeet — the Tiger of the Plains?

Back at Running Bear's camp, Broken Nose set up a shooting contest to see which of the three younger members of his party should have the extra gun.

At first Sun Boy refused to try for it, saying that Eagle Child was his more-than-brother who had saved him from the white buffalo bull. Anyway, was not Eagle Child their Chief's son?

But Broken Nose firmly insisted that prowess alone should decide the issue. To the surprise of everybody, moody and unpredictable Slides-to-the-Ground won the contest. But Broken Nose was not unhappy at the outcome. This left Eagle Child and Sun Boy with bows and arrows. They were the best bow marksmen in the tribe. There would be need for the bow and arrow to get meat when a gunshot might betray them to an enemy.

Eagle Child knew he had shot poorly. But he was finding it hard to keep his mind on what he was doing. He was still seething from his encounter with the white man, and he knew that this was wrong. He could almost hear his father, Night Rider, telling him it was wiser to let your mind dwell on the present than to worry unduly about things that were past, or things yet to come.

After holding council with Running Bear, the three older men decided they would leave their pack horse with the latter. The animal would only hinder them.

"Until we are well clear of Big River, we will move at night and sleep by day," said Broken Nose.

"A Blackfoot should not have to hide in Blackfoot country," Red Quiver grumbled.

"A wise hunter does not reveal himself to his quarry," Woodpecker retorted.

"And we will not always be in Blackfoot country!" Broken Nose nodded. "I, for one, expect to ride back on a Crow horse."

Eagle Child grinned to himself. As long as he could remember, Woodpecker and Red Quiver had always taken opposite sides in any argument. It was their way of masking a deep affection for each other.

But he was thrilled at the idea of going on a horse raid.

5

MAROONED

While Broken Nose's party rested during the long day, the women of Running Bear's band collected old lodge covers and thongs to bind logs for rafts to float the travelers' gear across Big River.

"Sun has only just passed the center of the blue," Eagle Child grumbled to his friends. He was eager to be gone. Like the other young men, he found it hard to settle down and rest as Broken Nose and the older warriors were doing.

Even Sun Boy found the waiting hard. In his role as the party's spiritual leader he had gone off by himself to see if he could get a vision of what lay in store for them. But the vision failed to come. He could only conclude that all the visions had gone to their Medicine Man, Wolf Calf, when the latter had prayed for the party's success during the sweat lodge ceremony before they left.

"When we have been gone for seven suns you will begin to get visions," Slides-to-the-Ground consoled him. "Once I heard Wolf Calf say this." Slides-to-the-

Ground was proud of his friendship with a future Sun Priest.

Darkness found them at the water's edge, several miles below Running Bear's camp. During the day, three of Running Bear's men had floated the rafts down and cached them near the mouth of a small creek. Each man of Broken Nose's party carried his weapons, a supply of pemmican for emergency rations, a sleeping robe, several pairs of extra moccasins and a repair kit. The last consisted of an awl, some sinew thread and extra pieces of skin for patching. They would travel two to a raft, and each raft would be in charge of one of the older men.

While Slides-to-the-Ground was helping Woodpecker load their raft he clumsily slipped and went into the water up to his waist. He gasped at the shock of the cold.

"Cold Maker must live in Big River!" he exclaimed.

"Ho!" scoffed Woodpecker loudly. "When I was a young warrior we would swim Big River without any logs to hang on to."

"After the Moon of Ripe Berries you swam it when Big River was so shallow a man could walk across," Red Quiver observed cynically.

Broken Nose told them to be quiet. Although all of the land across the river was considered Blackfoot territory, enemy parties were often found there, especially during the spring hunting season.

"The night has many ears," he cautioned. "When we near the other shore we must make as little noise as possible."

Each small raft was tied to the others by a thin strand of rawhide so the party would not become separated. Dressed only in their breechclouts, they slipped into the cold water, one on each side of a raft.

Eagle Child, too, gasped at the first shock of the cold. But he soon became accustomed to it. Kicking backward with the silent thrust their people had learned long ago by watching the antics of Old Croaker in the marsh ponds, they moved out onto the river.

"It is bad that we must cross when Big River is swollen with the Backbone's melting snow," grunted Broken Nose, who swam beside him.

How wide Big River is! Eagle Child thought to himself — much wider than it appeared from the heights above. He remembered how his brother, War Bonnet, had crossed alone five summers ago to rescue Antelope Runner from the Crow. He vowed that when the test came he too would not be wanting in courage. Halfway across, they began to run into difficulties as the swirling current swept them together. The rawhide ropes which connected each raft now became a nuisance. When one of the rafts almost overturned, Broken Nose told them to cut loose. "If we get separated, we will meet where Yellow River joins Big River," he said. They were to thank Sun and all the Above Ones for this later. It probably saved their lives.

Eagle Child and Broken Nose found their raft suddenly caught in a strong current which moved them rapidly away from their friends. Before the other rafts reached this bit of fast water, Broken Nose and his young companion were nearing the far shore.

"Close by is a deep coulee with many trees," the Head Scout said in a low tone. "It will lead us from the river to the high country where we can observe the land ahead for many buffalo arrows."

Now they felt their feet touch the bottom. It was one of the countless sandbars which form and then wash away to re-form elsewhere. Wading slowly, they eased the raft in toward the bank. Then they had to swim again for a short way because the sandbar suddenly disappeared under them.

Night Light chose this moment to come out from behind a cloud. Although this aided their landing, Broken Nose did not think it was a good omen.

When Eagle Child began to drag the raft up on the shore, the older man stopped him.

"We will unload it in the water," he said, "then we will set it adrift. We do not want anyone to know of our coming."

"Might we not need it for the return journey?"

Broken Nose shook his head. "We will come back another way. If the Above Ones approve, we will be riding horses."

Eagle Child had just pushed the raft back into the river when suddenly a fusillade of shots rang out from the bank above. A numbing blow on his shoulder sent him reeling backward. He heard wild, triumphant shouting, then Broken Nose grabbed him and they sank under as rifle balls ripped the surface all around them.

The cold water revived Eagle Child. When they came up again he found that Broken Nose was still sup-

porting him. Fortunately, Night Light had hidden her face again.

"I can swim," he gasped. They struck out rapidly from the shore — Eagle Child using only one arm. The other arm appeared to have no feeling.

Then their feet touched the sandbar again and they rested. Back on the shore they could dimly see dark figures moving around. There was a splashing in the water, followed by more triumphant cries.

Broken Nose cursed. "They found our raft," he muttered into Eagle Child's ear.

From somewhere along the shore a horse whinnied. The loss of their clothes and weapons so early in their journey was a bitter blow. The only weapons they now had were the knives stuck in the waistbands of their breechclouts.

"We cannot stay here," the Head Scout muttered. "If Night Light shows again the enemy will see us. Is your arm painful?"

"It feels as if Cold Maker had laid his hand on it," the younger man whispered.

"Later, it will feel as though Sun had touched it," Broken Nose told him. "But the water will clean the wound. If the bullet is still in your arm we will have to remove it."

Suddenly they heard a slight splashing noise fairly close by. Both Eagle Child and Broken Nose drew their knives and waited.

"If an enemy comes, sink into the water and come up under him," the older man whispered.

They heard the sound again, but this time they realized it came from the open river. In a moment Red Quiver, the best swimmer in the band, was beside them.

"What happened?" he whispered.

"Ambush," Broken Nose muttered. "The dog-faced Crow, I imagine. I couldn't see them. Where are the other rafts?"

Red Quiver pointed toward the deeper water. "They are bringing them in closer."

"We will swim out," said Broken Nose, looking at the sky. "Soon Night Light will again show her face and the enemy will begin firing. Already they have wounded Eagle Child."

They slipped away from the friendly sandbar. The two older men swam with Eagle Child in the center in case they should have to support him. In a minute or two, the dark shapes of the other rafts loomed ahead. They moved cautiously toward them.

Eager hands helped the wounded one to drape his good arm over a log of one of the rafts. Swimming strongly, the other five began to move the rafts back toward the middle of Big River.

They were none too soon. Night Light came on again in full force, turning Big River into a broad band of shining silver. There were excited cries from the shore, and several balls struck the water close by them. As the full current caught the rafts they picked up speed. But the shots continued for some time as the enemy followed along the shoreline.

"We must land soon," Broken Nose told Red Quiver, "or else the water will chill us. We must consider our wounded one, too." He indicated the other raft with a toss of his head.

"Perhaps this is an ill omen. Should we not cross to the other side and return Eagle Child to our people? Surely, the spirits are against us."

"Whoever the enemy are, they have invaded Blackfoot country," Broken Nose growled. "They took my gun, which I prized highly. I will make them cry for that."

"Are they on foot, or do they ride horses?" Red Quiver asked him. He too had no desire to turn back if this could be avoided.

"I heard a horse whinny soon after we reached the sandbar," the Head Scout said.

"Will they not search the shore at daybreak?" queried Slides-to-the-Ground, who had joined their raft to make room for Eagle Child.

"Not far below us the banks rise high. They would be unable to ride down to the river with their horses," Red Quiver mused. "In many places the brush is so thick we could lie concealed until the Falling Leaves Moon, if need be."

This sounded like a good idea to Broken Nose. If Eagle Child's wound turned out to be serious, he would have one of the other men raft him across the river. Eagle Child could then return to Many Houses where their band would soon be camped. The gunshot wound could be cared for by Running Bear's women. It was said, too, that the trader at Many Houses knew much about such things.

"We still have three guns and our other weapons,"

he nodded. "If the enemy are few they may be sorry they came looking for a fight!

"Look!" said Red Quiver. "We are nearing the high banks now."

Ahead they could just make out the dark, somber shape of a high butte against the lighter hue of the sky. Looking back, they could see that the raft bearing Woodpecker, Sun Boy and the wounded Eagle Child was not far behind.

"I will swim back and tell them," Slides-to-the-Ground volunteered, and disappeared into the darkness.

Broken Nose and Red Quiver began to tread water, checking their raft's speed in the hissing current. In a few moments the other raft caught up to them.

"How is your arm?" Broken Nose asked Eagle Child.

"There is not much pain." But the leader noticed that the wounded youth could barely keep his teeth from chattering. It would be wise to get in to shore where they could take a look at that arm, he told himself.

Sun Boy spoke from beside Eagle Child. "I have some powder that Wolf Calf gave me. It is good medicine for gunshot wounds. Some long ago Sun Priest made it from the flower of the sagebrush and other herbs."

They were well past the first of the high bluffs now. Woodpecker and Slides-to-the-Ground held the rafts together so that the party would not become separated.

"We will drift just a short while longer," Broken Nose said. Looking up at the group of stars called

Seven Persons, he could see there was still a long wait before daybreak. By the time it got light he wanted to have his party well hidden.

Night Light showed her face briefly under the veil of the overcast. Just ahead, a short bar of sand jutted out into the racing current.

"Behind the bar will be quiet water," Red Quiver said. "Let us go ashore there."

Broken Nose grunted assent.

All of them — even the stricken Eagle Child — kicked vigorously. Slowly they edged the two rafts in that direction. As they swept past the end of the bar their churning legs propelled them into the sheltered spot behind it.

While Red Quiver and Woodpecker sprang ashore to reconnoiter their surroundings, the rest of the party pulled the rafts in. Sun Boy helped Eagle Child up onto the narrow triangle of shore. With a weary sigh, the latter sank to the ground and rested while his friends unloaded the two rafts.

When Night Light came again, Sun Boy examined Eagle Child's wound. "Ho!" he said cheerfully. "The ball did not lodge there. It only passed through the flesh."

Hearing this, Broken Nose grinned with relief.

"Passing through it robbed me of my strength," muttered Eagle Child, but he was glad to hear that the wound was not serious.

"You are weak because you have lost much blood," Broken Nose consoled him.

Rummaging in his pack, Sun Boy removed a small

buckskin pouch. Undoing the thong which held it, he poured some grayish powder into the palm of his hand. Then he stepped down to the river and moistened the powder with water. He worked it into a fine paste. This he rubbed gently over his friend's wound, singing softly as he rubbed.

"In two suns the pain will be gone," he said with confidence. Then, seeing Eagle Child shiver, he fetched his own shirt and leggings and insisted the other put them on.

"This will mean that you will have no clothes," Eagle Child protested.

"Tonight I will wrap in my sleeping robe. When Sun comes up who will need clothes?" All of them had rolled their packs in light sleeping robes.

Broken Nose left them for a moment. When he came back, he had Red Quiver's robe around his shoulders. "Later we can make crude robes from the skins which cover the rafts," he said.

Red Quiver, Woodpecker and Slides-to-the-Ground returned to say they had explored the heavy thickets which covered the little shelf of level land under the high bluffs. Slides-to-the-Ground was rubbing a leg bruise he had sustained in a fall.

"The only way to reach here from above is to climb down the cliffs," Red Quiver grinned.

"The enemy could come by Big River, as we did," Sun Boy pointed out.

"Whichever way they came, they would soon wish they hadn't," Woodpecker said grimly.

"If we are quiet, and do our work well, they will

never know we are here," said Broken Nose. "First, we will take all our belongings into the heavy thickets under the cliffs. Then we will remove the covers from the rafts and push the rafts out into the water so that Big River carries them away."

There was a chorus of dismay at this. "That will mean we are trapped here with no way of escape," Woodpecker grumbled.

"For one who boasts of the time he swam Big River, escape should be easy," Red Quiver chuckled.

"It is useless for us to try to hide if we leave the rafts out for the enemy to see," Broken Nose explained.

"He is right," Red Quiver nodded. "Once they knew we were here they could rake the thickets with bullets. Some of us might get hit. It is better that we leave no trace of our landing."

When everything had been moved into the thickets, Woodpecker and Slides-to-the-Ground quietly edged the two rafts into the water. Silently they watched the current take hold of them and bear them far away. Then all but Eagle Child took willow branches and carefully erased all the marks they had made on the shore.

6

TRAPPED

Broken Nose awoke suddenly to the light touch of a hand on his shoulder.

"Seven Persons says that dawn is near," said Woodpecker, who had been on watch.

Quickly he aroused the others. As dawn broke, a deer wandered down and began to drink quietly at the river. Broken Nose cursed softly.

"If the deer scents us it will run. Any watchers above will wonder why it shows fear."

Sun Boy reached for his bow. "It is not yet full light," he whispered. "One well-placed arrow and the deer will not be able to warn anyone."

Broken Nose thought for a moment, then shook his head. It was true the fresh meat would be welcome, but trying to kill the deer was too risky.

To their relief, the animal finished drinking and wandered slowly away from them upriver. Sharing some of the pemmican from the four packs, they settled down to await developments.

Eagle Child found that much of the pain had gone from his wound. But the arm was stiff when he tried to move it. Looking at the wound in the daylight, Sun Boy was well pleased with his handiwork. He was glad Wolf Calf had given him the magic powder.

"Our long-ago people were good at wound healing," he said.

Broken Nose was pleased too. But he secretly credited the long soaking in the river for the wound's being so free of infection.

Somewhere above them on the high bluffs a horse whinnied. The Piegans froze in their positions lest a single movement of a branch or twig betray them. Broken Nose was glad now they had not shot the deer.

"I can see them," muttered Woodpecker, without turning his head.

"Who are they?" Broken Nose asked quietly.

"They are a long way off. But I think they are Parted Hairs from the far away country where Sun rises."

Broken Nose grunted incredulously. It was not often the Sioux came raiding this close to the Backbone. If this were so, they would have to be doubly careful. The Sioux was a clever and resourceful enemy.

"How many do you see?" he queried.

"Four riders," the other told him.

"Four," muttered Red Quiver. "Had we known, we could have ambushed them and taken their weapons."

"There may be others within the sound of a gun-shot," Broken Nose said softly. "They will have spread out so as to search far down the river."

"They have dismounted and are looking down here," Woodpecker told them.

"What if they should climb down to search these bushes?" Slides-to-the-Ground whispered.

"Then we will wait until they get within range of an arrow and take careful aim."

"It is better we should not talk," Broken Nose advised. "If a man talks, sooner or later he will forget and make a movement."

As they waited in silence, the impatience of the young men grew. Just when Slides-to-the-Ground was about to ask another question, Woodpecker spoke softly.

"They are getting back on their horses. Now they are riding away."

"I am thirsty," said Eagle Child.

"I will bring you water from the river," Sun Boy told him, starting to rise. The older men had not made a move.

"Stay where you are and be still!" Broken Nose hissed.

After a moment, Woodpecker spoke again. He was grinning to himself. "I see four heads on top of the bluff."

"It is an old trick," the Head Scout grunted.

"They have gone again," reported Woodpecker a short while later.

"We will wait a little longer," Broken Nose said.

A flight of crows passed above them winging in from the river to alight on an ancient pine that stood, gnarled and twisted by the elements, like a sentinel on the rim of the high bluffs. Broken Nose watched the birds for a moment. When they showed no signs of alarm, he nodded.

"We can move now."

Sun Boy went down to the river's edge and filled a skin bag with water. Eagle Child took a long drink, then splashed some of the water on his face.

"I feel better," he said.

"Well enough to travel?" Broken Nose asked.

The young man nodded. "If we do not go too fast."

"Good," the Head Scout grunted. "It is wise that we leave here. We will head away from Big River and re-join it far below the big bend."

"The Parted Hairs will follow the river," agreed Red Quiver. "It will be safer farther in."

As an extra precaution, Woodpecker was sent up on top of the bluffs to look for enemy signs. When he re-turned, he reported that the bluffs could be scaled quite easily at one point where many handholds were provided by overhanging bushes and rock outcrops.

"On top is a dead tree, which I climbed," he told them. "I could see no Parted Hairs for many buffalo arrows around."

They moved off slowly with Woodpecker in the lead. His feet encased in a pair of moccasins lent him by Sun Boy, Eagle Child walked behind Broken Nose. His left hand clutched the raft-cover skins which the Head Scout carried slung over one shoulder. It was a long way up. Eagle Child felt weak and giddy by the time they had reached the top. But his head cleared again after a short rest.

"You will soon grow stronger," Sun Boy assured him.

"When we return to our band the wound scar will be a badge of honor," Slides-to-the-Ground said. There was even a note of envy in his words. He would have welcomed the chance to win acclaim. Nobody ever took him seriously.

"We will travel until Sun lies directly overhead and then we will rest again," Broken Nose told them.

High noon found them climbing the steep slope of a bare finger of rock which stood up above the rough and rolling countryside. To the north, they could see the great bend of Big River with the Bear Hand mountains rising beyond. East of them lay the low rugged hills around Yellow River — their immediate destination. To the southwest a high square butte and a smaller dome-shaped hill stood between them and a range of wooded mountains. Many scattered herds of buffalo grazed quietly in the valleys.

A cry from Woodpecker halted them as they neared the top. He was pointing to the north. "The Parted Hairs!" he said.

Shading their eyes with their hands, his friends looked in the direction he had indicated. They could just make out the figures of four riders moving up a narrow valley that ran from somewhere below them in a winding northeasterly direction to Big River. If the strange riders kept following their present course they would eventually pass close to the Piegans' hiding place.

"We do not know they are the Parted Hairs," Red Quiver grunted. "They are too far away to be sure."

"They are four, and the horses look the same," Woodpecker said defensively.

Broken Nose shrugged. "It matters little. On top of this rock is a low spot large enough to conceal us all. No one will be able to climb up without being seen."

"Perhaps we do not need to hide," Woodpecker suggested. He swept his hand around the horizon. "They are four and we are six. I do not see any more riders from here to Big River."

Broken Nose paused in his climbing to consider the matter. Then he nodded slowly. "Perhaps if two of us showed ourselves we could lead them into an ambush. Last night on the river they saw only two."

Red Quiver shook his head. "They would have seen the other rafts on the water. They know your raft carried two men."

"Then why didn't they wait until we were all on the shore?" Woodpecker demanded.

"They fired when I started to push our raft back into the water," Eagle Child told him. "Perhaps they thought we had heard or seen something which made us suspect an ambush."

"If they knew we numbered six, why did they send only four warriors to search for us?" Sun Boy wondered.

"Maybe it is a small war party," Slides-to-the-Ground offered.

"A small war party of Parted Hairs should have more sense than to draw attention to itself in Blackfoot country," Woodpecker grumbled. "Perhaps they seek to join the spirits."

"We will send out no decoys," Broken Nose said. "If they come this way we will conceal ourselves and then attack."

They continued on up the slope. At the top, they found the low spot Broken Nose had spoken of. Somebody had made a windbreak of loose rock at one end.

"They are still headed in this direction," Woodpecker reported. "But they have slowed their horses to a walk. Sun will be halfway down before they arrive."

"Good," said Broken Nose. "We will rest before we fight."

Leaving Slides-to-the-Ground to watch the approaching enemy, the others stretched out on the rocks. Eagle Child was glad of the rest for his shoulder had started to throb.

"Warn us when they are within twelve buffalo arrows," the Head Scout told Slides-to-the-Ground. "That will give us time to go down and prepare a surprise."

The next thing Eagle Child knew, Slides-to-the-Ground was calling to them in some agitation, shaking each one in turn.

"They have stopped below us!" he said excitedly. "Two of them have started to climb this hill."

Broken Nose cursed him roundly. "Did I not say to rouse us when they were still twelve buffalo arrows away?"

Slides-to-the-Ground looked ashamed. "Sun warmed the back of my head so that I felt drowsy and closed my eyes," he said lamely.

"A lookout who sleeps becomes a nothing person," Broken Nose snapped. "Soon no other warriors will travel with him for they will not feel safe in his hands."

"Sun will be angry that you should blame him for your own weakness," Sun Boy told him severely.

Slides-to-the-Ground looked crestfallen. He had hoped to distinguish himself on this journey but he had succeeded only in putting his friends in danger and offending Sun.

"The two Parted Hairs are still climbing," Woodpecker reported a moment later.

Broken Nose cursed again. "They are coming up here so they can see far across the country, as we did. Now two of them and all of the horses will get away."

The other five inched forward on their stomachs to join Woodpecker. Broken Nose had taken Slides-to-the-Ground's newly acquired gun, leaving him with only his bow and arrows. Sun Boy had his hunting bow, but Eagle Child had nothing but his knife. Small chance he had to avenge the wound in his shoulder, Eagle Child thought bitterly.

"Let them get close enough so you can get them with your first shots," Broken Nose told the older men softly. The Head Scout held his gun in readiness for a snap shot in case one of his friends missed.

The climbers came steadily on; both of them were young and well muscled. Each carried a gun and a pouch of ammunition. They were Sioux right enough.

"Not yet," Broken Nose hissed as he saw Woodpecker's finger begin to tense on his trigger. He was happy that the Sioux had guns. His party had lost one, but if this skirmish went well they would gain two.

"NOW!" he cried suddenly.

Both shots rang out as one, echoing like thunderclaps in the thin, dry air. One of the enemy fell and lay still. But his companion let out a yell and darted behind a rock.

The two Sioux down at the bottom sprang to life. Spreading out, and taking advantage of every piece of cover, they began to work their way up the hill.

"If they can pin us down here until help arrives it will be our end," Broken Nose growled. "We must trick the Wounded One into exposing himself for a shot."

Red Quiver nodded quickly. He felt guilty because it was his shot which had failed to find a vital spot.

As Broken Nose sighted his gun at the rock which sheltered the wounded enemy, Red Quiver placed a moccasin on one of Sun Boy's arrows and slowly raised it above the rim of the hill.

A ball whistled past the moccasin. But the sound of the shot was lost in the blast of Broken Nose's gun.

The watchers let out a cry of triumph as the limp form of the enemy warrior slipped down beside the rock.

"Get those guns!" the Head Scout snapped. "Soon the others will be close enough to shoot!"

Red Quiver leaped over the rim and down the slope. Slides-to-the-Ground was hard on his heels. Both were determined to redeem themselves.

Shots rang out from below but they fell far short of the mark. In a moment the two Piegans were back, each clutching a gun and a pouch of ammunition.

Broken Nose let out a cry of delight when he saw that one of the guns was his own that had been seized with his raft.

Now there was no sound or sign of movement from the two enemy warriors below. They had taken cover hurriedly.

"We cannot stay here long," Broken Nose said. "We must make them think that we are many so they will go for help."

Spreading out along the rim of the hill they waited for a signal from the Head Scout. All but Eagle Child had guns now. He had armed himself with Sun Boy's bow.

At a nod from Broken Nose they all jumped up shouting and discharged their guns. Five shots panged off the rocks below, far short of the place where the enemy had last been seen. The two Parted Hairs sprang out from behind their cover and ran for their horses.

"They are fleeing!" Slides-to-the-Ground cried gleefully.

But the watchers on the hill soon saw that their strategy had not been completely successful. Only one Sioux rode off toward the west. The other sat on his mount quietly for a moment, then began to move slowly away.

"What is he doing?" Sun Boy asked.

"He is going to keep riding around our position to see that we don't escape," Red Quiver told him.

Broken Nose nodded gloomily. "We are much worse off than we were before. The other Parted Hairs will come more quickly now with someone to lead them here."

The Head Scout looked toward a large grove of trees many miles to the south. It was too far away to reach undetected. The same features that made their rocky hideout a hard place to attack made it also a hard place to sneak away from. For some distance around them the country was bare of cover. If they left the hill, the mounted man would follow them at a discreet distance, leaving a well-marked trail for his friends to follow. If they stayed, they would soon run out of water.

Yes, they were trapped, and there did not seem to be much they could do about it.

7

THE PRISONER

Eagle Child — who had been watching the circling rider for some time — suddenly had an idea. The enemy's horse was moving along at a slow walk. His owner, slouched in a leisurely attitude in the saddle, was giving the animal its full head. The horse appeared to be following the same path each time around.

"Below us is a rock big enough to conceal a man," he said to his companions. "See how he passes this rock each time he circles? I could reach that rock and get behind it while he is on the other side of our hill."

"You are wounded and still weak from losing blood," Broken Nose told him. But the idea appealed to the Head Scout. This son of Night Rider's appeared to have some of his father's skill at war.

"The wind is from the Backbone. The horse would fail to scent anyone who hid behind that rock," Red Quiver pointed out.

It was decided to send Woodpecker. He was a swift runner, and one of the best shots in the band.

As soon as the enemy rider rounded the west end of their hill, Woodpecker was over the rim and jumping

THE PRISONER   63

nimbly down the rocky slope. Sun Boy remained on the far side to report on the enemy's position. With bated breath, the rest of them watched their friend's progress. It was a long way down and across the open ground at the bottom to the shelter of that lone rock.

"The Parted Hair is almost halfway around," Sun Boy warned. The watchers groaned.

Woodpecker had not even reached the bottom of the hill. There would not be time for him to cross that open stretch before the other came in sight.

"Wait!" Sun Boy cried excitedly. "The Parted Hair has dismounted to tighten his saddle girth."

The faces of the others broke into smiles. Woodpecker had reached the bottom now and was racing across the open stretch toward the rock.

"The Parted Hair is up again. Soon he will come around the end of the hill," Sun Boy reported.

With a sigh of relief they saw that Woodpecker had gained the rock and managed to conceal himself in time.

The enemy rider had rounded the hill now. He was still following the course which would take him close to the rock where Woodpecker waited.

"We could fire so as to distract him," Red Quiver suggested. He was afraid something might go wrong with their plan and Woodpecker would be killed.

Broken Nose shook his head. "It could startle the horse so that he moves away from the path he has been following."

They waited tensely for the action to unfold below.

"He will have one, possibly two shots. But no more,"

Red Quiver muttered. He and Woodpecker had been through many battles together.

The Sioux was close to the rock now. They saw the figure of Woodpecker slowly rise from behind it as he prepared to fire.

Suddenly they saw the puff of smoke. Before the sound of the shot reached them, they saw the enemy's horse rear up suddenly, spilling its rider onto the ground. The frightened animal panicked and ran.

As the Sioux fell, his gun went flying into a clump of sagebrush. But the man was on his feet again instantly. Drawing his knife, he advanced toward Woodpecker warily.

With a wild shout, Red Quiver went charging down the slope to his friend's aid. The rest of the party followed more slowly, carrying the packs so they would not have to return for them again.

Below them, the two antagonists faced each other. Unable to reload his gun, Woodpecker had grasped the weapon by the barrel so that he could use it as a club.

The fight was over long before any of them got there. At the first pass of the knife, Woodpecker stepped nimbly aside and brought the stock down with a vigorous sweep calculated to cave his enemy's skull in. The Sioux just managed to get his head out of the way. The blow landed on his neck close to where it joins the shoulder and he fell to the ground.

Red Quiver arrived just as Woodpecker was retrieving the Sioux's gun from where it had fallen. The other four were close behind.

"Did you kill the Parted Hair?" Slides-to-the-Ground panted.

Woodpecker nodded, indicating where the Sioux had fallen. They went over to examine the latter's body. Just then the Sioux stirred and groaned.

"You will have to kill him again," Sun Boy grunted. "This one has two lives."

Suddenly the Sioux sat up, looking around in bewilderment.

"Bind him so that he can't escape," said Broken Nose. "He might be able to tell us something."

The Head Scout tossed them a piece of rawhide rope he had saved from the raft bindings. They soon had their sullen captive trussed up like a travois pack.

Broken Nose signed to the Sioux that he would not be harmed if he answered a few questions. How many warriors were in the war party that attacked them? Where was the main party located?

But the Sioux just ignored him.

Red Quiver drew his knife. "Perhaps we can make him change his mind."

"It would take too long," Broken Nose said. "My eyes tell me he is a proud man and a seasoned warrior. We must leave at once or his friends will overtake us."

"Let us leave him for Sun to punish," Woodpecker suggested.

"It is for Sun to decide who he will or will not punish!" Sun Boy reminded the older warrior.

"We can take him with us," Eagle Child suggested. "Maybe he will tell us how many white men have come into the land of the Parted Hairs. It is better to kill a man than leave him without food or water."

Broken Nose nodded thoughtfully. They had been told to learn as much about the white man as possible.

"Untie his feet so that he can walk," he said.

They set out for the distant trees in single file. Their captive traveled between Red Quiver and Woodpecker. A length of rawhide rope ran from the Sioux's bound wrists to each of the two Piegans.

They had been walking for some time when Broken Nose halted them beside a rocky outcrop. While the Head Scout and Woodpecker climbed up to reconnoiter, the others sat and refreshed themselves with a drink from one of the skin bags they carried. Their captive was still secured to Red Quiver.

Eagle Child held a bag up so their prisoner could have some. The man's eyes showed his gratitude.

"Why waste water on a Parted Hair," growled Red Quiver.

In a moment, Broken Nose and Woodpecker slid down to join them. They had disturbing news.

"Far away there are riders," the Head Scout told them. "I think they are headed in this direction. It is hard to say at that distance."

Slides-to-the-Ground looked worried. It had been his job to travel a few paces behind them to rub out any noticeable tracks they made. He was already responsible for much of the trouble they were in.

"The ground was dry and hard. We left no tracks that I could see."

"The enemy would guess that we might head for the woods," Sun Boy reassured him.

Broken Nose nodded. "We must turn and head toward Big River."

Eagle Child, who had been looking at their captive, saw the man's expression change ever so slightly and wondered at it. He could not understand what they said, but he must have sensed their concern and guessed the reason.

"Sun is far down in the blue," Woodpecker observed. "Soon it will be too dark for them to follow."

Red Quiver had now risen with the prisoner. "We could kill this one now and save ourselves a lot of trouble," he grumbled.

Woodpecker picked up the other end of the rope which secured the Sioux and they moved off.

Before following, Broken Nose called the younger men to him. He indicated where their captive had been sitting. A little marker of loose rock pointed in the direction they were now headed.

"We should kill the Parted Hair, as Red Quiver suggested!" Slides-to-the-Ground said hotly.

Broken Nose shook his head. He was angry too, but his anger was directed at the two older Piegans because they had failed to see the sign before starting off with their prisoner. Stooping down, he carefully scattered the rocks with his hands.

"The Parted Hair must have made it behind his back with his fingers while he sat there." Sun Boy was more interested than angry.

But the incident disturbed Eagle Child. How could the Sioux have known they would be changing their course toward Big River? Had Broken Nose pointed when he told them they must head that way? He did not think so.

"I would like to give the Parted Hair a clout on the head to teach him a lesson!" Slides-to-the Ground felt guilty that he had not noticed the rocks.

"Then he might suspect we have found this and make another," Eagle Child said quickly. "After dark it will be harder to watch him. It is better that we do not even mention this."

Broken Nose looked at his chief's son thoughtfully. He too was beginning to wonder at the Sioux's uncanniness.

"We must rejoin the others," he nodded. "We will say nothing to anyone."

The Head Scout did not intend that his party should be burdened with a prisoner for long. If they failed to get any information from him, Broken Nose knew of a friendly Gros Ventre village about one day's journey to the south where he could exchange the Sioux for some badly needed clothing and moccasins.

When darkness fell they stopped in a narrow ravine which was studded with a heavy growth of trees and bushes. They were delighted to find that the ravine also contained a small pool of clear, cold water which was supplied by a spring that bubbled out of the ground. For food they used the last of their pemmican.

"We will sleep until Night Light climbs well up into the blue," Broken Nose told them, "then we will move on."

Eagle Child was assigned to watch the prisoner until the moon came up, then he was to waken Sun Boy. The Head Scout had decided that Red Quiver and Woodpecker should be excused of this duty because they had had the captive all afternoon.

Long after the others had fallen asleep, the young Piegan sat staring into the darkness. His shoulder was still a bit stiff, but the wound appeared to be healing well. He wondered if this trouble which had befallen them so early in their journey meant that Sun frowned upon their efforts. He hoped that Sun Boy would soon be able to establish contact with the spirits so they could learn the wishes of the Above Ones.

He sat up, suddenly alert. Had he imagined it, or did the prisoner make a move? He watched the dark figure intently for a moment. Probably the man was just shifting his position, he decided.

Just when he had begun to settle back again, their captive spoke.

"You are right to worry about the white man," he said softly in the Blackfoot tongue. "Each year brings more of them into our land beyond where Sun rises, even into our sacred hills."

"Ha," thought Eagle Child, "now the mystery is explained."

Moving in so that he sat only a few paces in front of the other, he said aloud.

"Where did you learn to speak our tongue?"

"A north trader came to live with us who had traded with your tribes for many years."

"You say there are many white men in your country. What do they do there?"

The other shrugged. "They come for furs and for buffalo, and for the yellow rock. It is said that where they find the yellow rock the white man sweeps over the land like a flood."

"Do they come in the rolling lodges?"

"Many do," the captive nodded, "but more and more now come by Big River. Far from here they have great lodges which float on water. We call them fire boats because they make big smoke."

"Ho!" said Eagle Child scornfully. "Not many white men come as far as Blackfoot country!"

"They will come," the other told him, "and when they do they will claim the land for their own. The white man does not share. He takes and takes until there is no more."

"Then they will have to fight the Blackfeet."

"They will fight when they are ready," the Sioux said soberly, "for the present they are content to talk. Our chiefs say white men live in great numbers in the far far country. They have guns of many shots that don't have to be reloaded."

"My father once had a gun that could be loaded from the back," Eagle Child told him.

"These many-shots-guns are much more deadly than the guns which can be loaded from the back," the Sioux said. "The white man has these and many more. Already our old chiefs have signed a treaty."

"We too have signed a treaty," said Eagle Child. There was a trace of shame in his tone.

"Then soon you will see many white men on Blackfoot land," their captive assured him.

"Why did *you* come on Blackfoot land?"

"We were on our way to the country of the Pierced Nose Ones beyond the Backbone to get more of the spotted horses," the Sioux said evasively.

More likely on your way to get Blackfoot horses, thought Eagle Child. But he said nothing.

They lapsed into silence.

"I am thirsty," the captive said after a while.

Eagle Child placed his gun carefully against a rock. Then he rose and got one of the water bags that had been filled with cool, fresh water from the spring.

As he leaned so the other could drink, he suddenly felt himself jerked forward. Flashing lights exploded in front of his eyes as a hard blow caught him on the side of the head. He sank into unconsciousness.

When he came to, he found Sun Boy staring into his face anxiously. The other members of the party stood around in a circle.

"The Parted Hair . . ." gasped Eagle Child, attempting to rise.

"I was coming to relieve you just as he ran off into the bushes," Sun Boy told him. "I followed for a short distance, but lost him in the darkness."

"It was wise that you did not fire a shot," Broken Nose said approvingly. "His friends are mounted. They could be closer than we think."

"He has taken Eagle Child's gun and powder," Red Quiver observed.

"It was his own gun and powder," Eagle Child pointed out. His head still throbbed, but he felt better.

"We are lucky that he didn't sneak up and kill us one by one," Woodpecker said.

"He didn't have time," Sun Boy told him.

"I said he should have been dealt with," Slides-to-the-Ground muttered. "Now he will count coup on Eagle Child."

"We don't have time to stand here arguing," Broken Nose said shortly. "We must leave at once. Many buffalo arrows from here is a favorite camping place of our friends, the Entrails People. There we can obtain clothing and food."

He was annoyed that the enemy warrior had been able to retrieve his gun. These young men of his had so much to learn about prisoners.

8

♦ ♦
♦

THE RESCUE

At dawn they reached a stream which meandered
northward through a narrow valley. They were de-
scending a ravine when a deer leaped out suddenly
from behind some bushes.

Quick as a flash, Eagle Child flipped an arrow into
his bow and shot. The arrow hit the deer cleanly behind the shoulder just as the startled animal began a
leap which would have carried it to safety. Pierced
through the side, its body continued to roll down the
slope until it lodged against the trunk of a stubby poplar.

The others cried out in delight. They had not tasted
fresh meat since they had left Running Bear's camp on
the far side of Big River.

"We will stop and eat," Broken Nose said, nodding
with approval.

Eagle Child grinned proudly. His action had started
his shoulder throbbing again, but this was a small price
to pay for the feeling that he was no longer a drag on
the party.

"I'll go back and keep a lookout for Parted Hairs,"
Woodpecker said.

While Red Quiver skinned and butchered the deer,
Slides-to-the-Ground set about making a fire. He was
careful to collect only the driest of the dead branches
and twigs so that he could get a quick, hot blaze with
little smoke.

Eagle Child was sitting with his feet in the cold water
of the stream when Broken Nose joined him. The sun
had come up, and with it the first heat waves that her-
alded a warm day.

"Where is Sun Boy?" he asked the Head Scout.

Broken Nose pointed to a dense grove of willow

some distance away. "He has gone to seek the advice of the Above Ones," he said.

It was hard to get used to the idea that his friend and boyhood rival was a Sun Priest, Eagle Child mused. Of course, Sun Boy was not a full-fledged priest yet. But someday he would replace Wolf Calf as spiritual leader of the band.

"Is it far to this village of the Entrails People?" he asked Broken Nose.

"It is at the foot of the mountains where Yellow River divides," the other said. "We should reach there long before Sun reaches the middle of the blue."

While Red Quiver roasted a hindquarter of meat, the others rested. Eagle Child told Broken Nose what their captive had said about the white man's penetration of Sioux country. At last Red Quiver announced the meat was roasted.

"I'll go and get Sun Boy," said Eagle Child.

Broken Nose stopped him. "It is not right to interrupt if he talks with the Above Ones. He will come when he is ready."

Red Quiver was just getting up to relieve Woodpecker when Sun Boy joined them. His face was very worried.

"You had a vision?" Eagle Child asked him.

The other shook his head. "I had no vision, but suddenly I felt fear. Something told me that we must leave this place at once."

"Here, eat some fresh meat," Red Quiver grunted, handing the other a joint. "It is hunger you feel. Woodpecker has called no warning."

But Broken Nose had risen and was waving Woodpecker in.

"It is not right to disregard the warnings of the spirits," he said. "We have rested long enough."

When Woodpecker splashed across the stream to join them they asked him if he had seen any signs of the enemy.

"For many buffalo arrows back the land is empty," he said in an aggrieved tone. Woodpecker was a little annoyed that he would have to eat his meal on the run. As he talked he chewed vigorously on a piece of meat, determined to get some food inside him before they started off.

"The Parted Hairs are mounted. They travel quickly," Broken Nose reminded them.

"Sun Boy says he feels we are in danger," Red Quiver told Woodpecker. But his tone said he did not think much of Sun Boy's warning.

"He had a vision?"

Red Quiver shook his head.

Woodpecker sniffed. Like Red Quiver, he could not forget that Sun Boy had been just a child a few winters ago, although a very smart one.

Hearing them, Eagle Child reflected that his friend had a long way to go before the older people in the band accepted him as a Sun Priest.

"I felt that we should leave," Sun Boy insisted stubbornly.

"He has endured the seven tents of medicine," Broken Nose pointed out. "That gives him wisdom beyond his years."

They climbed from the valley with the Head Scout in the lead. Everyone carried a joint of meat to cook at their next stop.

Suddenly Woodpecker cried a warning. The others looked in the direction he pointed. Below them a group of horsemen had rounded a bend far down the creek. The newcomers were headed upstream, riding slowly.

"Are they Parted Hairs?" Broken Nose asked.

"I think so," Woodpecker nodded. "It is too far to be certain."

"They rode directly for the creek," the Head Scout nodded, "thinking to find our trail where we crossed. Come, we must seek cover quickly!"

The Piegans had done their best to wipe out all signs of their campfire. But Broken Nose was sure the sharp eyes of the Sioux would pick up some sign and guess the direction in which they were heading. For one thing, the sand that covered the hot ashes of their fire would be very warm. If one of the enemy should happen to touch it. . . .

They crossed the rim and were out of sight of the riders. The Head Scout quickly took stock of the country which lay before them. What he saw did not reassure him. For many miles the surface was unbroken by rocky outcrops or clumps of trees and bushes which might provide them with cover.

"When the fox is pursued he doubles back on his pursuers," he said. "We will follow the rim of the valley downstream until we have passed these riders, then we will conceal ourselves."

Red Quiver nodded. "If they are Parted Hairs on enemy land they won't have time to search the whole country for us." Turning northward, they broke into an easy trot.

Some time later, Woodpecker, who was keeping tabs on the progress of the enemy, joined them to report that they were now downstream from the riders.

Broken Nose grunted with satisfaction. He headed his party for a grove of gnarled trees. Slipping off their packs, the Piegans spread out among the sparse undergrowth and lay down to rest.

"It is well that we heeded the message from the Above Ones," the Head Scout observed. He did not say any more. But the others knew that from now on no move would be made without a consultation with Sun Boy.

When they looked at the young Sun-Priest-to-be their glances showed a new respect. They settled down to wait until they could see what the enemy was going to do.

"Next time I travel in enemy country I'll bring my horse," Slides-to-the-Ground grumbled to Eagle Child.

The latter nodded agreement. Yes, it would be nice to be sitting on Sun-in-the-Morning right now. He would not have to worry about any Parted Hairs.

"I have gone often into enemy country on foot," Woodpecker muttered. "In all my journeys I have never had the bad luck that we have had this time. Always I have crossed Big River without being seen."

"Perhaps the Above Ones do not favor this journey," Red Quiver observed soberly.

Hearing him, Broken Nose stirred uneasily. This was the second time Red Quiver had made this remark. Broken Nose was a stubborn man, but not a foolish one. No sensible leader would go against the spirits.

Their prisoner had told them much about the white man's doings in the sunrise country. Perhaps they should turn back now before a greater disaster befell them.

Woodpecker's voice broke in on his thoughts. "The Parted Hairs have left the valley!"

Peering out from the undergrowth, they could see that the group of riders had emerged from the breaks and were surveying the rugged terrain east of the creek.

"They have not found our trail," Red Quiver said with satisfaction. "They left the valley much farther downstream than we did."

"I count twelve riders," Slides-to-the-Ground noted. "A Piegan should be equal to two Parted Hairs."

"These are mounted Parted Hairs," Eagle Child reminded him.

"Why do they seek us?" Sun Boy wondered. "If they came to raid horses, why do they bother to chase a foot party?"

"Perhaps they think we still have our prisoner," Eagle Child suggested. "I talked with him for some time. He seemed to be a man who would stand high in the councils of his people."

"You talked to him too much," Red Quiver grumbled.

"I don't think they intend to seek further," Woodpecker observed. "They are just sitting in their saddles talking."

Then the watching Piegans let out exclamations of dismay. The mounted men had suddenly swung about and were heading north at a brisk trot — right toward the grove of bushes which sheltered them!

Broken Nose felt his heart sink. This was the final stroke of ill fortune that he had been afraid of.

"Do not shoot unless you must," he hissed. "They may pass right by."

On came the riders, closer and closer. The Piegans could already feel faint vibrations of the hoofbeats. Under Broken Nose's silent direction they spread out so that each crouched behind a tree which would shelter him when he stood up to fire.

Suddenly the enemy gave a chorus of excited cries and broke into a gallop!

"Somebody showed himself!" Red Quiver said with disgust. Why had he volunteered to travel with young untried warriors, he asked himself bitterly.

"Wait until they reach the very edge of the trees," the Head Scout cautioned. "If every shot tells, we can cut the odds so they have to meet us man to man."

He was not worried so much about Eagle Child, the only man of his party who did not have a gun. The Chief's son could flip a dozen arrows into his bow by the time the others could reload.

"They are not coming here!" Woodpecker cried. "Look!"

The oncoming riders had altered their course slightly

to the left. And the Piegans soon saw the reason. An Indian man and his woman, leading a horse-drawn travois of deer carcasses, were striving desperately to reach the shelter of the bushes.

Broken Nose saw that the charging Sioux would pass close to the edge of the trees which concealed them. He grinned to himself. Unaware of their presence the enemy would expose his flank to them.

"They don't even know we are here," he chuckled softly. "Fire into them as they pass."

The mounted warriors swept by in a swirl of dust. Suddenly the pounding of the hooves was lost in the thunder of Piegan guns. Several saddles were emptied with the first volley. The enemy scattered in confusion. Unable to gauge the strength of this new foe, they beat a hasty retreat in the direction of the creek. Soon the last of them had passed from view.

Shouldering their packs and weapons, Broken Nose and his men stepped out from the trees and moved toward the man and woman who still crouched behind the travois, as if in a daze. The Head Scout gave the sign of the Piegan Blackfeet.

The stranger stood up, much relieved. It was clear that he and his woman had never expected to survive. He signed that he was a Gros Ventre.

"I am Sitting Elk," he said, "and this is my woman, Spotted Calf. Our camp is far from here — where Yellow River divides."

Broken Nose nodded. "We were headed for your village. We have suffered much from those Parted Hairs."

He indicated his makeshift clothing. "We need some moccasins, shirts and breeches."

The other grinned widely and pointed to the bodies of four dead Sioux. "I would think the Parted Hairs have done some suffering too."

While they were examing the bodies, an argument arose over whose bullets were responsible for three of the fallen foe. There was no question of the fourth for he had an arrow clean through his body.

Picking up the dead man's gun, Broken Nose handed it to Eagle Child. "Perhaps you will be able to keep this one," the Head Scout said dryly. "They say a man values something more if he has won it himself."

Eagle Child flushed as he accepted the weapon. He knew the older man was referring to his clumsiness in losing the gun of the captured Sioux.

But Broken Nose slapped him on the back good-naturedly. The leader was quite happy at the turn of events. All his men had guns now. The three extra ones would make a handsome gift which would ensure their welcome at the Gros Ventre camp.

After they had taken their trophies, the Piegans joined their new friend Sitting Elk and his woman for the trek to Yellow River.

9

◆ ◆
◆

THE DEATH CAMP

AFTER their visit to the Gros Ventre camp of Sitting Elk's people, they traveled five days and finally came to a narrow river which snaked its way back and forth between low, rocky outcrops.

"South Bear River," Broken Nose told them. "We are in the home country of the Crow. From now on we shall sleep while Sun is traveling across the blue, and travel only when Night Light comes."

"Ha!" scoffed Red Quiver. "There is no enemy near. Two buffalo herds we have passed and even the cows with young calves were quietly eating the grass."

"An enemy party on foot could have traveled upwind of the herd as we did," said Woodpecker, as usual always ready to argue the point.

Broken Nose carefully surveyed the country around them for several moments. The wind from the mountains had dropped to a mere breath of air which barely ruffled the new prairie grass. To the east a small herd of buffalo grazed peacefully. With them were several keen-eyed antelope. These would be the first to bolt at any disturbing sight or sound. West of them a band of deer browsed the bushy slopes of a rock-strewn ridge. It was true that he and his friends had seen no unusual signs on their journey down through the gap between the little mountains.

But the south was an unknown quantity. Across the river their view was obscured by rough outcroppings of rock and brush. And south lay the whole Crow nation, always alert for signs of enemies in their midst.

"We will stop, and cross South Bear River after darkness falls," he told them.

None of the others was inclined to argue the matter further. It had been hot on the plains that day. Concealing themselves on a wooded rise, they settled down for a well-earned rest.

While they lay gazing skyward, Eagle Child noted a flight of marsh fowl winging toward them from the north. They veered sharply away as they neared the grove, then continued southward. His eyes followed them across the river. Crossing a ridge on the other side, the birds swerved suddenly again before they finally disappeared from view.

He looked quickly at Broken Nose to see if the other had watched their flight. The Head Scout returned his gaze and nodded.

"They could have seen the sudden movement of some animal. But it could also be a Crow camp."

Eagle Child now saw the wisdom of Broken Nose's decision to travel only at night. This would mean that they would cover less ground. But they had come too far to court disaster at the hands of some hunting party.

There could be enemy warriors concealed on that ridge across the river just as he and his friends were lying under cover here. If so, he wondered if he and his friends had already been seen.

A cry from Woodpecker alerted them. "Dust!" The sharp-eyed warrior was pointing to the east.

It was a dust cloud all right, and it was advancing along the river toward them at a steady pace. The Piegans crawled a little farther up the rise where the undergrowth was heavier, and waited.

"A herd of buffalo," Red Quiver snorted, "that is all!"

"You have lived for so many winters and learned nothing," Woodpecker said sadly. "Can you not see that the dust cloud is long and narrow like many riders traveling in single file."

"It is too heavy a cloud for riders," Red Quiver retorted. "To see and not to think is not to see at all."

"Perhaps it is more rolling lodges of the white men," Slides-to-the-Ground ventured. And for once that errant young man was right.

As the wagons began to come into view, the watchers could see that there were at least thirty of them. They were following the north bank of the river where the land was fairly level and covered with a heavy carpet of grass. Small bands of buffalo scattered as the wagons approached.

"If they keep on they will pass within one buffalo arrow of us," Red Quiver observed.

"Why would they not keep on, when they but follow

the trail of other rolling lodges that have gone before," Woodpecker grunted.

Looking toward the river, the others saw that Woodpecker was right. Scanning the grassy bottom-land closely, they could see where two parallel ruts or grooves followed the riverbank. So many white men had come that their wagon wheels had cut a road westward across this little-traveled country which served as a boundary between the Blackfoot and the Crow. This was news indeed.

Eagle Child remembered the words of their Sioux prisoner just before the latter escaped. "The white man does not share with anyone. He takes and takes until there is no more." The young Piegan felt a stab of foreboding. There would be much to tell his father when he returned.

The wagons were beginning to pass them now — the dust-choked wheels groaning in protest under their heavy loads. Unlike the quiet passage of an Indian band, the white man's progress was marked by much shouting and cracking of long whips.

"They would never be able to surprise an enemy," Red Quiver said contemptuously. "They move like a herd of buffalo."

But Eagle Child noted that keen-eyed men in buckskin rode in front and along the flanks. They reminded him of the white man his father and Wolf Calf had held council with before the spring buffalo hunt. Men who were wise in the ways of their people, as Night Rider had said.

He reminded Broken Nose of this meeting.

The other nodded. "Those men were wanderers. But these white men travel with a purpose, as if they know where they are going."

"Perhaps they carry only goods to trade for skins," Slides-to-the-Ground said.

"Or supplies for other white men who have gone before," Sun Boy added.

"You have had a vision of this?" Broken Nose asked eagerly.

Sun Boy shook his head. "The spirits will tell me nothing."

Broken Nose looked disappointed. It was easier to make plans when the Above Ones lent a hand. But one thing was certain — the white man was growing more active through the country along the Backbone.

As the long wagon train disappeared from view, Woodpecker suddenly let out an exclamation, and pointed.

"The Crow!"

Across the river, about twenty horsemen had ridden into view. There was no mistaking that neat, roached-up hairdo so beloved of the Crow.

The Piegans watched their ancient enemies in glowering silence.

Finding a shallow spot, the Crow riders urged their mounts into the river. They splashed across with the water coming no higher than the horse's knees.

"Perhaps they saw us come," Slides-to-the-Ground suggested.

Broken Nose shook his head. "This ridge would have

hidden our approach. They are spying on the white men."

The truth of this was apparent a moment later when the Crow party swung west in the tracks of the wagon train.

"We should cross South Bear now in the daylight," said Red Quiver. "We are still two suns' travel from Elk River where most of the Crow camps lie."

"The Crow does not stay in one place," Woodpecker reminded him. "He moves his camp after the buffalo as we do."

Broken Nose looked thoughtful. It was true there could be Crow camps almost anywhere. But he recalled that the riders they had just seen appeared to have well-filled saddlebags as if they had come a long way.

"Do you feel any presence of danger?" he asked Sun Boy. He was thinking of when the Parted Hairs had almost surprised them as they were cooking a morning meal.

"I feel nothing," Sun Boy told him.

"The Crow has shown us where we can wade safely across," Eagle Child pointed out.

The Head Scout nodded. If they waited until darkness fell, one of these younger ones would surely stumble and drop his gun in the water.

"We will cross and find a place to conceal ourselves on the other side," he told them.

For three nights they had marched southward. Above them, the group of stars called Ursa Major was fading rapidly, telling them that day was coming.

"Seven Persons says the night will not last long," Woodpecker observed, as they halted for a moment.

"Then we must quicken our pace so that we can reach the timber which cloaks Elk River," Red Quiver retorted.

They had just passed through a heavy patch of sagebrush and come out onto the edge of a flat plain.

"I hope that we reach the river soon," Slides-to-the-Ground grumbled. "I thirst for a drink of cool water."

"My tongue has swollen so that it sticks to the top of my mouth," Eagle Child agreed.

"Out there are Crow warriors who thirst for our blood," Broken Nose told them wryly. "I know this place. Beyond this plain lie the river breaks, and below them a grassy bottom much favored by our enemies as a campsite. If we go on now, daybreak will catch us halfway across the plain."

His friends groaned. None of them looked forward to spending the day in the scanty shelter of the sage. But they saw the wisdom of their leader's words. They had come too far to risk everything by some foolish act. Reluctantly, they turned back into the brush and lay down. Sun Boy withdrew from the rest to see if the Above Ones would send him a vision.

Daylight came on rapidly, and with it the relentless heat. Ahead they could see the river breaks. Their spirits picked up when they made out a herd of horses grazing along the rim. This meant a Crow camp must be near.

"With luck we could all take horses there and be gone without being discovered," Slides-to-the-Ground said, little realizing how much better it would have been for them all if they had done this.

"Pack horses," Red Quiver sniffed. "The horses we want are down below."

They slept fitfully during the long, hot day. Sun Boy rejoined them about noon.

"You had a vision?" Broken Nose asked hopefully.

Sun Boy shook his head. "Sun is busy in the sky. Night Light and Morning Star have gone to rest."

Eagle Child nodded with approval. Wolf Calf himself could not have given a better answer.

"You feel there is danger?" Broken Nose persisted.

Sun Boy shrugged. "There is always danger. It is true I feel something, but I do not know what it is. I ask myself why we have seen no Crow riders out to guard those horses, and no clear answer appears."

"It is too hot to sit out on the plain guarding horses," Red Quiver grunted. "The herd could be watched as well from the shelter of the river breaks."

Broken Nose looked thoughtful. It was quite possible the Crow had men posted in the breaks. When darkness fell they would have to proceed with care. If his memory served him well, the camp would be on the grassy bottom some distance out from the trees.

It was almost dusk when Slides-to-the-Ground awakened them. For once, that awkward young man had not missed his cue.

"First we will go to Elk River to wash and refresh ourselves," said Broken Nose. "Then we will hide ourselves in the trees along the bank and wait for our enemies to sleep."

They crossed the grassy bottom-land well above the Crow camp. After drinking their fill of water and removing the grime of their long journey, the Piegans felt ready for anything. Soon, the darkness began to gather around them. Screened by the heavy growth of willow and poplar, they crept close to the camp.

"The Crow must be nothing people," said Slides-to-the-Ground. "Only a few tipi fires are glowing. Do they not visit from lodge to lodge and talk with their friends as we do?"

"Perhaps they have been killing buffalo and have wearied themselves with butchering and hauling," Woodpecker said in a low tone.

"Ho!" snorted Red Quiver. "With fresh meat in camp we would be feasting and singing!"

Broken Nose growled at him to keep his voice down. But the Head Scout wondered about this quietness himself. One or two dogs barked, but there were no voices — no shouting of children.

"Perhaps they prepare to move at dawn and have retired early," Eagle Child suggested.

"It could be as you say," Broken Nose nodded.

"I feel that something is wrong," Sun Boy muttered, "that we should leave this camp and go elsewhere."

Broken Nose looked at Sun Boy uneasily. "Is it the same feeling you had about the Parted Hairs? You feel that we should flee at once?"

The other shook his head in a baffled manner. "This is not as strong a feeling. I do not feel the same need for haste. This is not a good place, my senses tell me, but that is all."

"No camp of the Crow is a good place for a Blackfoot man," Red Quiver said dryly.

"We do not intend to linger here," Woodpecker pointed out. "We will be gone as soon as we can find good horses."

Broken Nose nodded. They had come too far to go home empty-handed. The longer they remained in enemy country the greater would be the danger. After all, Sun Boy had admitted that he felt no need for haste. Nonetheless, the Head Scout decided to move with extreme caution.

"Two will go with me into the camp to lead out some of the best hunters," he said. "The rest will climb above the river banks and collect some of the range horses."

While they waited for their enemies to retire for the night, each Piegan took his personal war medicine from his pack. Eagle Child and Broken Nose, who had lost these precious articles when they were ambushed on Big River, had substituted two medicine pouches they had found on the dead Sioux.

The Head Scout had declared that the war medicine of a slain enemy was the best medicine of all. But Eagle Child was a bit doubtful of this. If it was such strong medicine, why had the Sioux been slain?

As they painted their faces and donned their medicine, they softly crooned their sacred war songs. No true warrior would neglect this rite.

Broken Nose had intended taking the two older men into the Crow camp with him. Then he decided against it. If anything did go wrong he wanted an experienced man to lead the rest of the party home. He looked at his companions thoughtfully. Red Quiver was the impatient one, inclined to be careless, although he was a good man in action. But it was Woodpecker who would have to lead the younger men. The slender warrior was keen of eye and fleet of foot, and he had that most necessary gift — patience.

But which of the young men should he himself take? Not Sun Boy. He had the knack of sensing danger. And as Wolf Calf's understudy, he was much too valuable a man to lose on a mere horse raid. What about Eagle Child? The Chief's son deserved the honor, but had he quite recovered his full strength from the wound? If he got into hand-to-hand combat could he hold his own? There was another matter to consider too. Eagle Child had talked with the Sioux about the white man's progress. He would be the best one to carry this information back.

This left only Slides-to-the-Ground, the Head Scout thought wryly. There was nothing really wrong with Slides-to-the-Ground. He was a bit clumsy, and often let his feelings overrule his brain. But perhaps age and experience would cure this. There was another reason why it should be Slides-to-the-Ground. He did not have the status in the band enjoyed by the other two men. A coup like this could be the making of him. The Head Scout felt he had an obligation to see that Slides-to-the-Ground got his chance.

When Broken Nose announced the two scouts who would accompany him into the Crow camp, the faces of Woodpecker, Sun Boy and Eagle Child showed disappointment. But they accepted their leader's judgment.

It was decided that the three who entered the camp would carry nothing but their knives. Loaded with the extra guns and equipment, Woodpecker and the two younger men set off for the upper plain where the pack horses grazed. They wanted to reach the river breaks before the moon rose. If things went wrong in the camp, the others were to escape on foot and join them.

Just before the first moonbeams began to creep over the grassy bottom-land, Broken Nose stood up. "We will get ready now," he said quietly.

Collecting some cottonwood sap, they rubbed it on their arms and bodies. The cottonwood odor would quiet the picketed horses so they could be led away by strangers without making any fuss. Dogs would also find it harder to detect an alien presence.

They passed the first line of lodges without discovery. The Crow appeared to be sleeping the sleep of the dead. Small fires still glowed in a few lodges. But there was hardly a sound. Only a few horses were picketed by the tipis.

"This is a poor camp," Red Quiver muttered disgustedly.

As they passed one tipi they saw a fine pinto picketed in front of it. Broken Nose signaled to Slides-to-the-Ground. They crept silently toward the horse. Red Quiver went on to look for another.

Untying the pinto, Broken Nose placed the rope in his young companion's hands.

"Go to the foot of the breaks and wait," he whispered. "We will bring more horses out to you."

Broken Nose had decided it was too risky to let Slides-to-the-Ground poke around the camp on his own. It would be better to have him hold the animals they collected. Taking the pinto would be Slides-to-the-Ground's coup.

Slides-to-the-Ground moved to obey. Suddenly his eyes fell on a beautiful quiver covered with white fur which hung in front of the tipi. White skins were generally given to Sun. An offering like this would win him great prestige at the Sun Dance.

Then their ears caught a strange moaning sound. It was coming from inside the tipi. Curious, Broken Nose parted the skins and looked in. A horrible odor greeted him. The sight which met his eyes was even more horrifying. In front of the small fire, an old woman sat rocking forlornly back and forth. There were several bundled forms around her. She did not see him for her eyes were swollen shut. But it was the ugly sores which spotted the woman's face which sent Broken Nose reeling back in horror.

"The Spotted Sickness!" he cried. "Do not touch a thing!" he warned Slides-to-the-Ground. "We must leave here at once. Quickly, let the horse go! We must find Red Quiver!"

A dog that had come out to investigate these strange voices began to bark. Other dogs joined in.

"Come!" said Broken Nose impatiently.

Slides-to-the-Ground released the pinto's rope and turned to follow his leader. Again the white quiver caught his eye. For a fraction of a second he hesitated. Suddenly he reached up and grabbed it. Slipping the prize over his shoulder, he trotted after Broken Nose. The temptation was too great for him to resist.

They almost collided with Red Quiver, who was running to meet them. He had made the same discovery. The whole camp had the sickness. The older men who had been through a smallpox epidemic before knew the terrors of it. Running swiftly, they headed for the river breaks to tell the others. Slides-to-the-Ground kept to the rear so that his friends would not see the precious quiver bobbing in the darkness. Once he stumbled and fell. He felt the thorn of a brush graze his shoulder. But he picked himself up hurriedly and continued on.

10

◆ ◆
◆

A WILD STAMPEDE

Eagle Child sat on a vantage point above the river breaks. Woodpecker had sent him back to watch for the others so he could guide them to where the range horses were being rounded up. They had encountered no night guards.

The moon had risen now, bathing the bottom-lands in a soft radiance. The Chief's son could see the ghostly forms of the Crow lodges, and here and there the fading glow of a tipi fire. Somewhere a dog yapped, and the chorus was taken up by several others. Eagle Child tensed, fearing to see the whole camp come alert. But he relaxed when nothing further happened.

Suddenly his eyes caught a flash of movement at the edge of the camp. Three figures had detached themselves from the shadow of the tipis and were moving briskly across the open ground toward the breaks. He was sure they must be Broken Nose, Red Quiver and Slides-to-the-Ground.

Eagle Child's heart sank. The raiders had been discovered. He hoped that Woodpecker and Sun Boy had managed to catch enough of the range horses so they could make their escape in the darkness.

Getting up, he readied his gun so that he could check the pursuit with a well-aimed shot or two. When no pursuers appeared, he lowered his gun and waited. The three figures had reached the bottom of the breaks now and were climbing up toward him.

When the one in the rear stumbled and almost fell, Eagle Child grinned to himself in spite of the apparent gravity of the situation. Anyone could stumble, but he was willing to bet his newly acquired gun the rear runner was Slides-to-the-Ground.

As the figures neared the top, Eagle Child called softly in the Blackfoot tongue. Broken Nose answered him. When the latter came up, Eagle Child asked him what the trouble was.

"The Spotted Sickness!" the Head Scout said bitterly. "The whole camp appears to be stricken. But we touched nothing except the halter rope of one horse, and the flap of a tipi cover."

"I also touched nothing but a tipi flap," Red Quiver said.

Glancing at Slides-to-the-Ground, Eagle Child was puzzled to see that he had what appeared to be a quiver slung over one shoulder. The Chief's son was sure he had packed his friend's quiver along with his gun and other personal effects when he left with Woodpecker and Sun Boy to find the range horses. But he could have been mistaken, he told himself.

"What was the use of taking your quiver if you had no arrows or bow?" he queried.

Broken Nose and Red Quiver stopped in their tracks. They *knew* their young companion had carried no quiver when he had started out. Grimly they walked around the unhappy Slides-to-the-Ground. They peered at the offending object in the moonlight.

Red Quiver let out an exclamation of disgust.

"You took that from the sick camp," Broken Nose said accusingly. "I told you to take nothing."

"You are a fool!" hissed Red Quiver. "Once again you have put our lives in danger!"

"It is covered with the skin of a white badger," Slides-to-the-Ground said sullenly. "I wanted to keep it for a sacrifice to Sun. Would Sun let any harm come to those who make a sacrifice?"

Broken Nose was very angry. So great was his anger he could have throttled the culprit right there. He knew the disaster Slides-to-the-Ground's foolish actions could bring on them. But he choked down his anger and spoke with what patience he could muster.

"When people have the Spotted Sickness their skin flakes off. Sometimes the flakes are as fine as dust, and where this dust lands the Sickness spreads."

Slides-to-the-Ground felt a pang of fear. He knew that warriors rode stripped to the waist in the spring and summer hunting. The fur of this quiver must have been in contact with the owner's bare shoulder. With a cry, he unslung the quiver and tossed it from him. It disappeared into a nearby ravine.

"That will do no good!" Red Quiver snorted, "The skin dust is probably already on you."

Eagle Child indicated a nearby sandbank. "Take some of that earth and rub your body with it," he advised the crestfallen Slides-to-the-Ground.

"We should leave this unclean one to find his own way back to Blackfoot country," Red Quiver growled.

"Perhaps the three of us are unclean," Broken Nose said soberly. "There is no fear of pursuit from this camp. Before we leave we will all bathe in Elk River."

They marched up onto the plain with Slides-to-the-Ground trailing many paces to the rear. The Head Scout had insisted on this.

When they joined Woodpecker and Sun Boy they found the latter had collected six fairly good horses.

Broken Nose and Red Quiver told them how they had fled the Crow camp to avoid the Spotted Sickness. While Slides-to-the-Ground sat forlornly some distance away, his five companions held council to decide what their next move should be.

Broken Nose was all for letting the horses go and walking back home. He was convinced the Above Ones had been against this trip from the very start. Had the spirits not sent warning after warning?

"Soon the Above Ones will run out of patience," he told them.

Sun Boy was inclined to agree. "Remember the feeling I had that we should leave here," he said.

Red Quiver did not like the idea of walking home. He wanted to find some other Crow camp where they could get horses. But Woodpecker disagreed with him.

"We are weary of traveling," he grunted. "These horses have probably been grazing here since before the Sickness came. Let us mount them and head for Big River."

Eagle Child was as anxious as any to mount and ride for home. He was eager to see his family and his own pony, Sun-in-the-Morning. Counting the time spent in the Gros Ventre camp, they had been gone for twenty days.

It was finally agreed they would wash themselves and the six horses in Elk River and head for home. Broken Nose had insisted on this final precaution. And he refused to stay long enough for them to round up extra horses to take back with them. The Head Scout thought the spirits might cease to protect his party altogether if they continued to defy them.

They had traveled for two days without mishap when Slides-to-the-Ground's pony stepped into a badger hole. Horse and rider were sent sprawling. The others — who had been riding a little ahead of the disgraced one — drew rein and waited for Slides-to-the-Ground to get up. But he lay as if dead. His horse had risen and was cropping the wispy prairie grass, apparently unharmed.

"He has just had the wind knocked from him," said Red Quiver. "In a moment he will revive."

All of them were reluctant to go to their friend's aid because of their fears of the Spotted Sickness. Only that morning Sun Boy had noted that the scratch on Slides-to-the-Ground's back had turned an angry color. But this could be because of dirt in the wound, he admitted to himself.

"He moves!" Eagle Child said happily, as his friend stirred and then slowly sat up.

But Slides-to-the-Ground sank back again with a groan.

"What is the matter?" Broken Nose barked.

"My leg pains when I move it," Slides-to-the-Ground told them. The Head Scout looked at the two older men and grimaced. Here was more trouble. More than ever he was convinced that they should not have made this journey. They dismounted to consider the matter.

Red Quiver pointed to a thicket near where Slides-to-the-Ground had fallen. "Let him crawl into those bushes and wait for his leg to heal. We will leave him a water bag and some meat. We can tether his horse so it can graze, but not move beyond his reach. This we have done often for a brother who has been badly wounded."

For once Woodpecker agreed with him. "In a few suns his leg will heal so that he can crawl up onto his horse and ride home."

Like Red Quiver, he wanted no contact with the dread Sickness.

Broken Nose nodded thoughtfully. "Perhaps the Above Ones intend it to be that way." He was quite aware it would be several days before the smallpox signs would break out on Slides-to-the-Ground, if he had the disease. Perhaps the spirits had arranged this fall to protect the rest of the band.

Eagle Child and Sun Boy exchanged sorrowful glances. They were remembering the young Slides-to-the-Ground, companion of their childhood games.

They would have stood together in trouble then, and they had no desire to abandon their friend in enemy country now. Yet they could see the sense of the older men's thinking.

"I will stay with him while the rest of you go on," Eagle Child volunteered.

Sun Boy shook his head. As far back as he could recall, the lodge of Slides-to-the-Ground's family had stood next to his own family's lodge whenever the band made camp. Slides-to-the-Ground had always been his loyal supporter in everything he tried.

"I will stay with him," said the young Medicine-Man-to-be. "I will bind his leg with willow and help him to get on his horse. And only I have the healing powder for the cuts and bruises he received when he fell."

Red Quiver was quite willing to accept this solution. He was anxious for them to be on their way. But Broken Nose agreed only when he saw it would be useless to argue with Sun Boy. If any harm came to Wolf Calf's apprentice the Medicine Man would blame him for it, he told himself.

"Have care," he warned Sun Boy as the rest of the party prepared to ride. "If the Spotted Sickness comes, neither of you will be able to return to camp."

Sun Boy pointed to where the white rim of an alkali slough glinted at the bottom of a deep draw. "When I have put the injured one on his horse, I will go down there to the stinging water and wash," he said. "Wolf Calf once told me of a sick warrior who avoided death by washing himself in a slough that was rimmed with the white earth. Later he rubbed his body with blackened wood from his campfire to ease the sores."

Broken Nose looked doubtful. He had never heard of this cure. But it made him feel a little better that Sun Boy appeared so confident. Reluctantly, he gave the signal for the rest of them to move off.

Looking back at his two friends, Eagle Child felt a pang of foreboding. He wondered if he would ever see either of them again.

The following day they had to seek cover twice to avoid Crow hunting parties. Both times it was only a combination of good fortune and Woodpecker's keen eyesight which saved them. Now that they had crossed South Bear River, Broken Nose suggested they should head more toward the east instead of trying to go directly home.

"Too many buffalo herds are moving between here and Yellow River," he grunted, as they rested in a pine grove. "And where you find buffalo you will also find the Crow."

This was a disappointment. It would add many more miles to their journey. They had hoped to be well into Gros Ventre country by the third day, but the stolen pack animals had proved to be clumsy and slow. Even Red Quiver agreed they would have to keep well clear of Crow hunting parties. With mounts like these they would never be able to elude pursuit.

"We can go to where South Bear River swings north and follow it to Big River," Woodpecker suggested. "Then we can cross Big River and head toward the Bear Hand Mountains."

"Many parties of Cutthroats roam the other side of Big River," Red Quiver pointed out. Cutthroat was a nickname many Blackfeet used for their old enemies the Assiniboin.

But the plan appealed to Broken Nose. "Most of this route runs through the lands of our friends the Entrails People," he reminded them.

There was another good reason too. To the north and east the plains were dry and sandy, but if they decided to follow South Bear River they would always have fresh water, and an abundance of rich grazing for their horses.

Eagle Child stayed out of the argument. Being unfamiliar with the country, he was satisfied to leave the route to the others. Personally, he would have been content to choose the shortest way home and take his chances with the Crow.

As they rode on, he kept glancing back, hoping against hope that he would see Sun Boy and Slides-to-the-Ground appear. This is probably what saved them later, for he was the first to catch sight of the large group of riders bearing down on them.

Woodpecker identified the newcomers at a glance. "The dog-faced Crow!" he cried, digging his heels into the flanks of his horse.

His friends followed suit. As they pounded across a stretch of flat, dusty prairie, it soon became apparent that the superior mounts of the enemy would soon overtake the scraggy horses the Piegans had pressed into service.

Ahead lay a low, stony ridge. They swept over this

and were confronted with a large herd of buffalo grazing beneath.

"Ride into them!" shouted Broken Nose. "It's our
only chance!"

Snorting in alarm, the buffalo on the fringes of the
herd suddenly came to life. The four riders rode right
into their midst, scattering the shaggy animals before
them. Charging buffalo butted wildly into others of
the herd until the alarm and confusion spread for
miles. Thousands of the brutes started to mill around,
bellowing angrily. Great clouds of dust began to rise.

Eagle Child could barely make out the figures of the
three older men riding ahead of him. Desperately he
urged his mount forward in an effort to catch up. But
time and time again a charging buffalo would cause the
frightened horse to veer away until all sense of direction was lost.

Then a new sound began to force itself on his con-
sciousness. A low rumble which seemed to build up
rapidly with every passing moment. It was more of a
feeling than a sound. A frightening rumble that shook
the very ground under his horse's hooves.

Fear clutched at Eagle Child's throat. He knew only
too well what the new sound meant. The whole herd
was beginning to stampede down the valley, and he was
caught in its midst. Years ago, he had seen the tattered
remnants of a horse and rider that had been caught in a
runaway buffalo herd. A hurried glance to the right
and left confirmed his fears. The buffalo were all running in one direction now, bearing him and his horse
along like a piece of driftwood on Big River.

A frantic cow butted against them, sending his mount reeling. Dropping his gun, Eagle Child grabbed at the horse's mane. The animal regained its balance and plunged gamely ahead. They were safe for the moment, but the young Piegan knew that the tiring pack animal would not be able to stay on its feet for long.

Suddenly a low rock outcropping loomed through the swirling dust ahead. His eye caught sight of an overhanging tree, stunted and gnarled by the action of sun and wind. In the split second remaining to him, Eagle Child made up his mind. Slipping off his bow and quiver of arrows, he rose nimbly on the back of his plunging mount.

As the tree rushed toward him he held his breath and

leaped. The coarse bark tore at his hands, but he clung grimly on. There was a sickening crack and the old tree sagged, throwing Eagle Child against the face of the rock. Scrambling quickly, he pulled himself up and sank panting beneath a fringe of bushes on top.

All around him poured the plunging buffalo like a river in flood. The thunder deepened to an angry roar. Eagle Child put his hands over his ears to deaden the sound.

THE FIREBOAT

The next thing Eagle Child knew he opened his eyes to find that the sun was dipping below the mountains. Realizing that he must have fallen asleep, he raised himself cautiously on one elbow and looked around. There was not a buffalo to be seen, nor any Crow warriors for that matter. Feeling hungry, he reached for the little pouch of dried meat he carried tied to his waist. To his relief, he had not lost it when he jumped. Chewing the meat made him feel thirsty.

Somewhere close, a coyote yapped, and was answered by another a moment later. Eagle Child flattened himself against the rock, scarcely daring to breathe. Then his eye caught a flash of gray against the grass. A coyote loped across a slight rise to the west. Not far behind trotted a second animal.

Eagle Child grinned with relief. If the Gray Ones frolicked on the prairie no enemy riders could be near. He stood up and stretched his muscles, then slid down from his rocky perch. The first thing to catch his eye was the mangled remains of his gun — the second gun he had lost on this journey, he reflected ruefully. But he was thankful just to be alive.

Truly it must be as his people said. The spirit of the white buffalo must be following him to ensure that he come to no harm. He wondered whether his horse had managed to escape, or if it had been knocked down and gored by the pounding hooves. And what about his friends, had they too been able to reach safety?

With the sinking sun on his left, he set out across the plains. If he kept on in this northerly direction he knew he would eventually reach Big River. From there, he could find his way home.

A short time later he came upon the remains of his horse. But for a few scattered remnants of hide, he would have had a hard time identifying the unfortunate animal. Its lack of speed had been its downfall. Now, more than ever, Eagle Child feared for his friends. They were all mounted on poor horses.

As he straightened up from examining the dead horse, he heard the sound of voices. They came from somewhere quite near. Crouching low, Eagle Child peered into the deepening dusk. But he could see nothing. He waited with every sense alert.

Off to his right some shadows moved. As they drew closer, they formed three distinct figures — one large figure and two smaller ones. By the look of it, they would pass some distance from where he stood. But Eagle Child sank onto the grass, remembering that his tall form would be silhouetted against the western sky.

A horse snorted. Then the character of the three objects became clear. It was a horse-drawn travois attended by two persons. By their voices, both of them were women.

"Returning from a hunt with a load of hides and meat," Eagle Child nodded to himself.

That would mean a camp was close by. Was it a Crow camp, or a camp of those good Blackfoot allies, the Entrails People? It could be either, for he and his friends had crossed South Bear River yesterday.

It was very important that he identify these people, Eagle Child realized. If they were Crow he could steal a horse and win honor; if Gros Ventre, he would have to walk into the camp and ask for the loan of one. But he was pretty sure it would be a Crow camp. He had come only about eight buffalo arrows from where the Crow hunting party had surprised him and his friends that afternoon.

Rising to his feet, Eagle Child began to follow the retreating figures. He could just make them out in the gloom. He decided he would cross the trail of the travois and follow a parallel course to the east of it. There was still a bit of light to the west which might reveal him.

Then another thought intruded. What if the menfolk of these women should be following the travois a short distance behind? He stopped and listened intently. There was nothing but the steady clopclop of the single animal pulling the heavily laden poles. To make sure, the young Piegan placed an ear to the ground and listened for a telltale drumming of hooves that would signal the approach of a fast, high-spirited horse such as a hunter would ride.

Satisfied, Eagle Child arose and continued his stalking. The two women were not hard to follow for they were doing a good deal of laughing and talking. He made a mental note to instruct the women of his father's household in the dangers of making too much noise when traveling on the plains at night — if he got home safely, that is.

The dark line of a ridge appeared to the west and the travois seemed to be veering toward it. As they drew nearer, the line broke to reveal a narrow gap in the ridge where a small stream wound through.

Eagle Child stopped by the stream and had a drink. It was cool and refreshing. He was sure the travois was headed for this gap. That would mean the camp must be somewhere on the other side of the ridge, possibly at a widening of the creek bottom. If this were true, the gap would surely be guarded. His logic was rewarded a few minutes later when he heard a deep, masculine voice call out, and the women answer.

Eagle Child was almost certain they were Crow now for the words were unintelligible to him. He was familiar with the Gros Ventre tongue because it was much the same as the Blackfoot.

Passing to the north of the gap, Eagle Child began to move cautiously up the ridge, keeping his eyes alert for any signs of movement. Reaching the top, he slid down onto his stomach and began to slowly work his way over.

The first thing that greeted his eye was the glow of lodge fires. He counted about fifty of them. This band would be about the same size as his own — big enough to spare more than one warrior for lookout duty.

The next thing he had to find out was the location of any extra watchers. If the ridge were unguarded, he could then slip down to the camp's edge where he could observe some of the people moving about in the firelight. He had to make sure they were enemies.

Creeping far enough down so that he would not be silhouetted against the crest of the ridge, Eagle Child rose to a sitting position. For some minutes he let his eyes roam the slope to his left, pausing searchingly at every bump in the contour, at every deeper shadow. Whenever he encountered a change, his eyes remained fixed there until the object was either identified or judged to be harmless. The slope to his right received the same treatment. There was not a sign of movement anywhere.

Still Eagle Child remained where he was, completely motionless. He remembered the warning of Broken Nose earlier in their journey.

In the camp below a dog barked, then another and another. Here and there a voice was raised as some man greeted a neighbor. A vagrant breeze from the west stirred the grass at his side, bringing with it the tantalizing aroma of cooking meat. Eagle Child's mouth watered. Fresh meat was much more appetizing than pemmican.

Suddenly his ear caught the soft pad of footsteps somewhere on the ridge behind him. He flattened himself against the ground and waited. The dark figure of a man appeared. He was traveling down the face of the ridge at an angle which meant he would pass only a few paces from Eagle Child. The young Piegan crouched even lower.

But the newcomer's eyes were eager for the camp ahead. His thoughts were on the hot meal and warm sleeping robes which awaited him. For one brief moment the figure was etched against the camp glow before the man passed from Eagle Child's line of vision. No mistake about it, he had the fancy piled-up hairstyle of the Crow warrior!

Well, that much was settled. It was an enemy camp, all right. The only way he could get a horse would be to take one. Now there was no need to go down close to the camp until he was ready to act.

Eagle Child settled back for a long wait. He did not feel like attempting the coup while the camp was still awake. He would go when the fires died down and the people were drugged with the heaviness of those first hours of sleep.

The moon had risen, bathing the camp in a ghostly light. Eagle Child worried a little about this. Perhaps he *should* have gone in at dusk as some of the more experienced raiders did. He could have secured a horse, and then mingled with the people he had seen leading their animals down to water. But this was a small band. If anyone accosted him he would be spotted as a stranger at once.

Not a sound came from below. Remembering that he had been told it was best to rub the body with cottonwood sap when entering a strange camp, Eagle Child looked around. He could see what appeared to be the outline of a grove of trees on the far side of the camp, but there were no cottonwoods near him. Instead he collected a few sprigs of sage and rubbed his body and arms thoroughly. At least the dogs and horses in the camp would find this a familiar scent.

As he crept down the slope, Eagle Child wondered if these Crow kept an individual lodge watch as his own people often did. This would mean that members of each family with picketed horses outside their tipis would take turns at staying awake to listen for any unusual horse movements. If the warriors that had surprised them yesterday belonged to this band, the Crow would already be alerted to the presence of Blackfoot raiders in this area. He might be walking right into a trap. Perhaps he should be satisfied with another pack horse.

But Eagle Child discarded this idea with a shrug of impatience. He was tired of plodding along on a pack animal. He wanted a real horse under him which could move with the speed and agility of a deer.

At the first lodge he stopped for several moments and listened. One of the sleepers breathed with a deep rasping sound that made it hard to determine how many people were inside. But there was no horse picketed in front. Eagle Child moved deeper into the camp.

His eye was caught by a big dark horse beside a gaily decorated tipi. As Eagle Child moved closer the animal started nervously and jerked at its rope. The young Piegan retreated in alarm when he saw the lodge poles dance. He crouched in the shadow of a neighboring lodge and waited. Suddenly he saw the flap of the other tipi open and a man step out and look around. The man went over to the horse and quieted it. Eagle Child saw him examine the rope carefully, then give the horse a final pat and disappear back inside.

After this close call, Eagle Child decided he had better be satisfied with a pack horse. Moving silently on the balls of his feet, he headed for the other side of the camp where he had seen the pack animals grazing.

He had passed the last tipi when he heard the soft thud of hoofbeats behind him. Whirling in dismay, he saw that a black and white horse was following him. Relief flooded over him when he saw that the animal was riderless. The horse veered away when it sighted Eagle Child. But it stumbled and came to a halt abruptly. Eagle Child saw the trailing halter rope and grinned.

Approaching the animal cautiously, he picked up the rope. Then he moved to the horse's side and patted it soothingly. The horse appeared to be resigned to the fact that its bid for freedom had been thwarted. It nuzzled the young Piegan curiously.

Without further ado, Eagle Child swung up onto the animal's back and dug in his heels. In a flash they were away. He could hardly believe his good fortune. Pausing on the ridge where he had crouched in wait for the camp to retire, he listened. But he could detect no sounds of pursuit. Keeping well away from the gap where he had heard a guard challenge the two women, he headed northward.

Just before dawn, Eagle Child dismounted and led his horse into a grove of trees. Tethering the animal, he

ate the rest of the dried meat and then lay down for a short rest. As soon as it was daylight, he would look the whole countryside over and figure out the quickest route to Big River, he promised himself.

He was just beginning to settle down when he saw the bush where he had tied the horse begin to thresh around in a curious manner. Rising quietly, Eagle Child crept up beside the animal to find that it was working industriously away at the knot, and with great success. In fact, in another few moments the horse would have freed itself.

"I see that you are one of those clever ones," Eagle Child grunted. "Men who have such clever horses do a lot of walking."

He could possibly use part of the rope to hobble the animal's legs, but this might not work either. Finally, Eagle Child decided the only thing to do was to keep traveling. The horse was too valuable an asset for him to take any chances.

"I have heard it said that a horse like you is a bad spirit, sent back to earth to plague whoever owns him," he grumbled, as he climbed resignedly onto the animal's back.

With the coming of the day, Eagle Child decided to confine his travel to watercourses and coulees so that he could not be seen from afar. The plan was not without its dangers. If he could not be seen from a distance he could also not *see* any distance. There was always the possibility that an enemy could creep up on him undetected.

Partly from loneliness and partly from the habit he

had formed of talking things over with Sun-in-the-Morning, Eagle Child explained their position to the piebald.

"If we travel the coulees our route will be longer," he said, "but it will be smoother going."

The horse tossed its head as if to let his young rider know he did not care one way or the other.

There was little chance of getting lost. From now on, all watercourses would lead to either South Bear River or Big River. South Bear River joined Big River somewhere to the east. With luck, Eagle Child told himself hopefully, they would reach Big River by early afternoon. He hoped the piebald was a powerful swimmer.

"Sh, sh," he commanded, urging the horse to a faster pace. Then he remembered that a Crow horse could not be expected to understand Blackfoot, so he prodded the sleek flanks with his heels. The animal snorted in protest, but increased its speed until they were moving along at a fast trot.

Soon the sun appeared. As the early-morning rays warmed his shoulder. Eagle Child's spirits picked up. He broke into song, singing one of the war chants of his people.

If Wolf Calf had been there, the Medicine Man might have warned him that the Above Ones look on war songs as a prayer for the sight of an enemy.

As it was, he was quite unprepared for the six Crow warriors who came charging out of a branching coulee several hours later — just after he had joyfully sighted the rocky walls of Big River.

But Eagle Child recovered his wits quickly. With a

snap of the halter rope, he sent his mount into a gallop. Feeling the urgency behind his rider's commands, the piebald responded well, showing a surprising speed in those thick, powerful legs. To the Above Ones, the young Piegan breathed a prayer of thankfulness for sending this sturdy animal when he had been about to settle for a lowly pack horse.

Fortunately, the branch the enemy had ridden down was on the east side of the main coulee. Eagle Child had been riding close to the west wall so as to take advantage of all the shade that was offered.

Glancing over his shoulder, he saw that he would be able to pull ahead. By the time the nearest of his pursuers reached a point directly behind him, Eagle Child would be at least two buffalo arrows away.

The young Piegan realized that only two possible courses lay open to him. He could climb out of the coulee and head westward to Yellow River, hoping to locate that Gros Ventre camp he and his friends had visited, or he could keep right on for Big River. But Yellow River was far, far away, and he did not know how the piebald would stand up under a long chase. On the other hand, Big River offered no guarantee of safety either. Broken Nose had said there was fast water and many rocks in some places. If he *could* cross the river safely so could his pursuers. And once on the other side, how did he know he would not run into a party of the hated Assiniboin? He would land about halfway between the Wolf Mountains and the point where Little River joined Big River — a favorite camping spot of the Assiniboin.

Looking back again, he caught a glimpse of the leading pursuer through the billowing dust clouds. Did he imagine it, or had the Crow warrior narrowed the gap between them?

"If I headed west," he muttered, "I would be only part way up the side of the coulee by the time the Dog-Faced Ones arrived. I would be an easy mark for their guns."

There was no other choice but to continue on to the river and hope for a safe passage across.

The coulee opened suddenly. On they raced — a series of tiny dust clouds on a parched and level plain. An eagle circling high above watched them curiously. This was the only sign of movement in all his wide domain.

Reaching the river breaks at last, Eagle Child could see the smoky-blue Wolf Mountains beckoning on the other side. Beyond these, to the northwest, lay the beloved and familiar Bear Hands where he hoped to find the camp of his people. He felt a catch in his throat.

They slid down a narrow cut in a shower of loose shale. Eagle Child again breathed a prayer to Sun, Night Light and Morning Star. This time he asked that the black and white horse under him would prove a fast swimmer, and that the current would not be too swift.

Between them and the river lay a short stretch of sandy bottom-land — shifting and dangerous under the flying hooves. Several times the horse lurched as if about to fall, but those powerful legs churned on, bringing them safely through.

Eagle Child heard a triumphant shout from the

Crow as they too reached the breaks and saw that he was not too far ahead.

Then he and the piebald were splashing through the reviving coolness of the shallows. He had apparently come out below the rocky part of the river, for the bottom was sandy here. Out of the corner of his eye, the young Piegan saw that the leading Crow had almost reached the bank of the river. But Eagle Child's horse had struck deeper water now, and was swimming strongly for the other shore. He slipped off the animal's back, gradually working his way to where he could grasp its tail.

Suddenly he heard the warrior on the bank give a strange, piercing call. To Eagle Child's horror, the piebald swung around obediently at the signal and began to swim back. In desperation, the young Piegan let go of the tail and struck out valiantly for the distant shore.

Through his mind flashed Woodpecker's boast about swimming Big River. But even if this were possible, he knew the horses of the enemy would soon overtake him. His only chance then would be to seize hold of a horse and try to dispatch its owner with his knife. There was only a slim chance of success, but he was determined to give it a try. Often his father had said that a fight is not lost until hope and determination are gone.

Dimly he heard the sound of a gunshot, then another and another. Balls struck the water on both sides of him. The man who had called the horse would be its owner, Eagle Child told himself. This explained one mystery. The reason the man had not fired before was fear of hitting his own horse. But why had this warrior not pursued him into the river?

Snapping a quick look behind him, Eagle Child saw a sight which made him stop and tread water in amazement. All the Crow warriors were fleeing wildly away from the bank.

Suddenly a terrible sound smote his ears. Half moan and half screech, it was like nothing he had ever heard before. Turning in the direction of the sound, the young Piegan was swept by a wave of terror. A huge monster was headed his way, churning and frothing the waters angrily as it sought to reach him! Billows of

black smoke poured from two big black posts in front! Some terrible god of the water people, he thought wildly, come to devour him for disturbing its lair.

Then through his fear one scene began to register on his mind. At the front of this monster he could see the figures of white men moving about. Recognition dawned. This must be one of the great fireboats their Sioux prisoner had spoken of. Eagle Child heard a strange voice shouting, but he did not know what it said.

"That's an Injun in the water there!"

A melodious tinkling sound came to him. The boat's churning and frothing slackened. It became quieter, but still slid closer until it towered over him menacingly. The young Piegan's eyes bulged. He had never even dreamed of anything like this!

Suddenly he saw that a long pole had been thrust into the water beside him. A number of voices were shouting what appeared to be instructions. Half in a daze, he seized the end of the pole. To his horror, he felt himself being swung in toward what appeared to be a keel boat lashed to the monster's side. The pole slipped and he sank under momentarily, to emerge choking and gasping for air. A powerful hand grabbed one of his flailing arms and hauled him into the smaller boat. Now many hands were reaching down from above to clutch him. Eagle Child felt himself being drawn up over a big wooden ledge. By this time he had ceased to care what happened. All he wanted was to get out of the water where he could have a chance to recover his breath. Half fainting, he collapsed on what appeared to be a broad wooden floor stacked with boxes and cut lengths of wood. The floor trembled oddly. Strange figures crowded around, blotting out the friendly warmth of the sun.

But one thing puzzled him. In all the wonder of this new world, one of the voices that sounded in his ears had a strangely familiar ring.

SON OF A CHIEF

Eagle Child turned his face in the direction of the voice. A lean, dark face swam before his eyes and receded. Then the image cleared, and recognition came. This was the Tall One who wore the deerskin. Just before the Moon of New Grass, he and his father had watched while this man talked sign with Wolf Calf.

He raised his hand and greeted the man in Blackfoot. This action seemed to alarm some of the men around him, for they stepped back, talking excitedly.

"Look out! He may be dangerous!"

"Maybe we should tie him up!"

But a big, burly man — one of two important-looking men who stood beside the Tall One — waved them away. The former had a coat with brass buttons and an odd hat, much like that worn by Badger Head, the trader at Many Houses. Although he could not tell what was being said, Eagle Child sensed that this man was some sort of chief. Perhaps the smaller one was a medicine man for the others showed him a good deal of respect.

Then the Tall One spoke. "You had better treat this

fella pretty good if you figger to travel in Blackfoot country. He's a chief's son."

He returned Eagle Child's greeting in Blackfoot, and said that the fireboat's chief — pointing to the man in the dark coat — and the chief of many fireboats (indicating the other) bade him welcome.

"Ho," thought Eagle Child to himself, as he acknowledged the greeting. "The Tall One has learned much of our language in the short time he has been among us." But he understood now about the other two men. One held the same rank as his father, and the other was like Head Chief Many Buffalo.

As Eagle Child rose to his feet he became aware that the wooden floor under him was rumbling and shaking more violently than ever before. He clutched at the Tall One's sleeve.

"Is the fireboat angry?" he asked fearfully.

For a moment the man looked puzzled. The young Piegan repeated the question using sign to illustrate his meaning.

A glint of amusement appeared in the Tall One's eyes. "Where Big River runs swiftly the fireboat must work harder," he explained gravely.

Reassured, Eagle Child relaxed a little. This made sense. When he reached a swift point in the river did he not have to swim more vigorously?

Ignoring the curious glances of the people, Eagle Child looked around him. He understood about the boxes and sacks. These were trade goods for Many Houses and other forts the white man had built. He knew that the keel boats carried the white man's goods.

Being small, they just could not handle such a quantity. But the many lengths of wood stacked neatly about the boat baffled him.

"Why do you carry the wood of so many trees?" he asked the Tall One.

"The boat must have wood to feed on," the other told him.

Of course! This was a fireboat! It would need wood the same as the cooking fires of his own people needed wood. Somehow the white man had devised a way to make fire do the work of many men laboring with poles and paddles. Eagle Child's heart sank. There appeared to be no limit to the cleverness of these pale strangers.

Then another thought struck him. The fireboat was made of wood. If a hot fire raged somewhere inside the boat's house, why did it not consume the boat? What magic prevented the whole thing from going up in smoke? Eagle Child could not escape an uneasy feeling that the white man had somehow become possessed of a power that only the spirits should have.

"I would like to see the fiery heart of the fireboat," he said to the Tall One.

The man in buckskin looked at the boat's captain.

"He wants to look around a little."

The big man looked at the owner, who nodded briefly.

"That's all right. Just so long as you stick with him," the captain told him. "You're the only one who can savee his lingo."

"That Injun has a knife," said the owner. "Don't you think we should take it off him?"

"I wouldn't try it," the Tall One advised. "It might take a bit of doing."

Eagle Child looked from one to the other inquiringly. He sensed that the Tall One had asked the fireboat's chief if he could see the fire which burned somewhere below, and he had seen both chiefs nod in agreement.

As he and the Tall One made their way toward the house part, the young Piegan saw what appeared to be a small house perched on top of the main structure. This is where the chiefs sleep, Eagle Child decided. They passed a curious metal object. It consisted of a short, thick tube of iron with a large hole in it. When Eagle Child asked what it was, he was told it was a gun.

The young Piegan's face blanched. Then those big round balls lashed near it must be bullets. With a mighty gun like this the white man could be invincible.

Now he knew what he must tell his father. If he and his people were to survive they would have to learn to live with the white man.

On the way, they passed many men who appeared to be constantly carrying sticks of wood into the lower part of the house.

Eagle Child drew back when his guide stepped through a narrow doorway. The move was instinctive. This might be some sort of trap. But he followed quickly as the other beckoned, not wanting to show his fear. Once inside, he forgot all else in the amazement of what he saw.

In front of them, men were busily tossing more sticks of wood into a huge metal monster that puffed and grunted. Every so often their sweating faces shone in the glow of fierce fire which appeared whenever one of the men opened some sort of cover or lid. Eagle Child could feel the blast of the heat on his own face, and an acrid odor filled his nostrils.

He now saw how the fire could live in the heart of this wooden boat. It was contained in a great iron pot, built something like the cooking pots his people were getting from the traders. But the similarity ended there. This metal monster was alive! It had a great arm which threshed up and down!

Eagle Child drew back in alarm at a sudden hissing noise. The pit below became obscured in a heavy mist — hot and fearsome like the mists where hot water bubbled up out of the bowels of the earth in some parts of the Backbone. Gasping and choking, he felt his way back to the doorway and out into the clean air.

"The monster must be angry to smoke and spit like that!" he cried to the Tall One who had followed him out.

"The same thing would happen if you put a pot of water over one of your cooking fires and held down the lid," his new friend told him.

Then the Tall One led him back toward the rear of the vessel where most of the noise of the fireboat came from. Here Eagle Child saw a great circular object which spun around in the water with much thumping and gurgling, sending showers of spray in its wake. It appeared to consist of some sun-shaped disks such as the rolling lodges used. The disks were lashed together with flat poles.

The young Piegan grasped the function of this new marvel quite readily, when the Tall One described it as "many paddles." But he was unable to see the connection between the fire monster below and this great paddlewheel that drove the fireboat through the water — no matter how hard the white man tried to explain.

Finally, the man gave up and led his charge forward toward the bow. As they passed the moving lines of firewood again, Eagle Child wondered if there were enough trees along the river to feed a monster like this.

Once back at the familiar spot on the foredeck where he had first been hauled aboard, Eagle Child felt better. It was quieter up here. He could look ahead to the country of his own people, and away from these terrifying and confusing things which belonged to the white man's world.

Suddenly the boat gave a sickening lurch. Many of the boxes and piles of wood came crashing down. Eagle Child and the Tall One were thrown to the deck. But they jumped up again, unharmed. They had been too far forward to be hit by any of the falling objects.

"We're stuck on a sandbar!" the Tall One shouted.

He was answered by the captain and the owner, who came running out of the small house above. This confirmed Eagle Child's belief that the small house was a chief's lodge or a council house.

Although he could not understand what was being said, the young Piegan knew what had happened. The fireboat had struck a shallow spot in the river. It was not moving any longer.

Many men came running in obedience to orders

shouted from above. Then Eagle Child saw the reason for the long, flat boats which were lashed to the big boat's side. Instead of piling the boxes of goods up again, the men were loading them into the flat boats.

He looked inquiringly at the Tall One. The other scratched his head a moment before he answered in a blend of Blackfoot and sign. "If a pack horse is stuck in a marsh you take off its load so that it will be easier to pull out."

Eagle Child's face cleared. Many of the white man's ways were strange, and he was the possessor of many wonderful things, but he too must struggle with Big River, even as the Indian did.

The sun went down behind the hills and still the boat refused to move. Finally, the captain gave orders for them to cease their efforts.

"Maybe it's best to spend the night out here," he said to the Tall One. "No telling what we might run into if we tied up somewhere along the shore. While you're at it, ask that red-skinned friend of yours if there are any big Injun camps hereabouts."

When the Tall One put the question to Eagle Child, the young Piegan shrugged and said that he did not know.

"Ask him who was chasing him when we picked him out of the water," the captain growled.

The man in buckskin had refrained from asking this before because he thought it might be resented. As he struggled to present the question as tactfully as possible, Eagle Child answered it for him. He pointed to the south.

"A long day's ride from here is a camp of the dog-faced Crow," he almost spat the name. "It is they who followed me to the banks of the river."

The Tall One grinned to himself when Eagle Child told of the treachery of the black and white horse. "Do you think that is the nearest camp?" he asked.

Eagle Child shook his head. "This is the time when all people hunt the buffalo. There could be many camps close by. Many suns ago I visited a camp of our friends, the Entrails People, on Yellow River. They too hunt along Big River."

"How many suns ago?" the Tall One asked.

Eagle Child indicated thirteen with his fingers.

"What does he say?" the captain demanded impatiently.

"Those were Crows chasing him, and they're camped a day's fast ride from here. He says there could be lots of camps nearby. About two weeks ago he was at a Gros Ventre village on the Judith."

"You think the river will drop much overnight?"

The Tall One shrugged. "There are two high-water periods in these parts — one in April and one from June to early July. We could be nearing the end of a high-water period pretty soon."

"We'll rig 'er up for sparring and then sit here until morning," the captain decided. He left Eagle Child and the Tall One so that he could inform the owner of his decision. He found him supervising the loading of the flat boats, which river men called "mackinaws." Orders were passed to the crew to get spars ready.

With keen interest, Eagle Child watched them setting

up the spars. Two poles were placed in the sand, one each side of the bow. These were set at an angle, sloping toward the front of the boat, and each was connected by rope to a steam winch on the deck.

He signed to the Tall One that he did not understand what was going on. To him, the drumlike winch was another form of the curious round things which could paddle big boats and move the white man's rolling lodges.

"Rope Eater," the Tall One explained, pointing to the winch. Taking a small piece of loose rope from the deck, he gave one end to Eagle Child and clasped the other in one of his own hands. Using this hand as a spool, he wrapped the line around and around, allowing himself to be drawn closer to the young Piegan as he took up the slack. Then he made a motion with his arm supposed to represent the boat slipping up and over the sandbar into deeper water.

Eagle Child looked doubtful. It was hard to believe that the mighty fireboat could be dragged in this manner.

Once the sun had dropped behind the river breaks, darkness came on quickly. The Tall One tried to talk him into sleeping inside the deckhouse, but Eagle Child would not consider it.

"Out here I will be guarded by Night Light, Seven Persons and Morning Star," he told the white man.

The other nodded, understanding. He went inside the big, broad deckhouse and returned a moment later with roasted buffalo meat and some white stuff he called "bread."

Making himself comfortable in front of a stack of cargo, the young Piegan ate hungrily. The meat was fine, but he did not care for the bread so he tossed it away. Being tired from his exertions, he was soon asleep.

Eagle Child had no idea what had awakened him. Did a board creak somewhere, or had some instinct bred into his people through centuries of living with danger stirred his senses? He opened his eyes to a bright canopy of stars. Suddenly he blinked and looked again. It seemed as if one of the heavy cargo cases stacked above him was moving in his direction.

With an agile flip of his body he was on his feet. The heavy case came crashing down where he had been lying! With a cry of anger, Eagle Child slipped his knife from his belt. He was up and over the pile of cargo in two swift leaps, just in time to see a dark figure disappear into the shadows of the deckhouse.

Someone shouted from the little house above, and figures came running. The first to reach the foredeck was the Tall One.

"What has happened?" he asked Eagle Child.

"In the darkness an enemy came and tried to kill me," Eagle Child growled. The young Indian was seething with anger. "He pushed one of the trade boxes."

"Perhaps a Crow swam out from shore."

"It was a white man," Eagle Child said sullenly, pointing toward the deckhouse. "He hides in the fire-boat's big house."

By that time the captain had joined them. "What's the trouble?" he said.

The man in buckskin explained what had happened, then he added, "You don't want any of that kind of trouble. Next thing you know you'll be fighting a skirmish every time you land a woodcutting crew."

The captain nodded grimly. "I'll find who it was and fix him proper. You stay with your redskin friend and try to pacify him. The boss wants to build a freight run, not start an Indian war."

"The man will be found and punished," the Tall One said to Eagle Child. He indicated that they should return to the bow of the boat.

Eagle Child agreed with reluctance. He would much prefer to find this unknown enemy and confront him, but he realized this might prove difficult.

After a time the captain came out to where they sat. He conversed with the Tall One for a few moments and then returned to the deckhouse.

"It was a man whose brother had been killed by the Sioux," the Tall One explained.

Eagle Child shrugged. "If there is bad blood between this man and the Parted Hairs he should seek revenge on Parted Hairs," he said simply.

"He blames all Indians for what happened to his brother."

This was foolish, thought Eagle Child. There are good and bad Indians. But the young Piegan felt relieved. At least he now understood the reason for the attack. Yet he was amazed that anyone should think a

Blackfoot was no different from a Sioux. This was probably because white men themselves were so much of one kind, he decided.

They sat together listening to the waters of Big River swishing past the hull of the stranded riverboat until dawn broke in the eastern sky.

When the round, drumlike thing on the deck began to turn, Eagle Child saw why the man in buckskin had called it "Rope Eater." As the rope tightened it squeaked in protest. All at once the fireboat seemed to rise and hop forward. Crewmen rushed up and reset the poles. The boat lurched ahead again, getting closer and closer to the deeper channel.

Eagle Child now understood what the Tall One had been trying to describe the day before. The short, forward leaps of the boat reminded him of the big hopper bugs in the prairie grass.

The river appeared to be dropping rapidly. This seemed to worry the people of the fireboat. Do they not know Big River always does this, Eagle Child wondered?

Toward the middle of the day, the nature of the river changed. Sand gave way to rock and the silty waters ahead churned angrily around great boulders in the channel. They were close in to the north bank now.

The Tall One pointed to the cargo and then to the shore, explaining that they might have to leave half the load there while they took the rest up through the rapids, then make a return trip.

"Sometimes they tie a rope to a tree and Rope Eater pulls us through the angry water," he said.

White men are always loading and unloading things, the young Piegan thought wearily. This was woman's work. Eagle Child was getting a bit tired of being on the boat. He was not used to such a confining space. And there was always the danger of enemies. He had not forgotten last night's incident.

"I want to return to my people," he told the Tall One.

"You have no weapons," the man said. "You could run into Assiniboin hunters, or even a Crow war party."

Eagle Child laughed. Once in the timber of the hills he was sure he could elude any enemy.

The Tall One got up and walked toward the deckhouse. Eagle Child saw him stop and talk with the captain and the owner, who were leaning on the rail above. Then the plainsman disappeared inside the deckhouse.

In a few moments he returned, carrying a north trader's gun, a powder horn and pouch of bullets. He presented these to the amazed Eagle Child.

"Take them," the Tall One said. "It is a gift from the people of the fireboat."

The captain and the owner had thought this a good idea when the plainsman suggested it. They had had much trouble downriver with Sioux firing on the boats and raiding woodcutting parties. If possible, they would like to be on good terms with the mighty Blackfeet. Then there was that attempt on Eagle Child's life the night before. Perhaps the gun would help erase the memory of this.

Eagle Child was overwhelmed. He hefted the gun expertly, feeling the smooth stock.

"You are indeed my brother," he said happily.

Knowing something of these people of the upper river, the Tall One did not discount the value of this remark. He smiled and nodded.

As the boat approached the bank, Eagle Child and his friend scanned the breaks carefully for any sign of movement.

"When I reach the top I will wave if all is clear," Eagle Child told the Tall One, then he leaped ashore. The white men watched as he climbed nimbly.

"You think you can trust him?" the captain grunted.

"I would bet on it," the Tall One replied. "If he has friends up there they won't bother us. If he runs into enemies, he'll start shooting."

Reaching the top, Eagle Child looked back. The mighty fireboat did not look so imposing from up here. As far as he could see, there was no sign of any riders. A band of deer browsed quietly between him and the uplands. The young Piegan raised his arm and waved. Below, the Tall One answered.

Turning, Eagle Child headed for the distant Bear Hands where he hoped to find the camp of his people.

I 3

◆　◆
◆

DISASTER

A RIDER suddenly topped a distant rise to the west. Eagle Child watched as the stranger and his horse stood for a moment silhouetted against the setting sun. Was it friend or foe? The young Piegan knew he was somewhere near the northwestern tip of the Bear Hand mountains. The newcomer could well be one of his own people.

In a moment the rider continued his journey, heading directly for the ridge where Eagle Child lay concealed in a clump of bushes.

It had been a long journey up from the mighty rapids of Big River where he had left the Tall One and the others toiling with heavy boxes of trade goods. Eagle Child had counted eight suns since he had waved good-bye to the men of the fireboat.

His progress had been slowed by the need to hunt for food. Then it was necessary to dress and cook the meat. One whole day and a night had been spent in a small camp of friendly Gros Ventres, where he had been able to exchange a fresh deer hide for some new moccasins. Another day had been lost dodging a marauding party of Assiniboin. He had been forced to swing back toward the south in a wide loop. But at last he was close to where Broken Nose had expected to find their band's encampment.

The rider was much closer now. His course would take him along the base of the river where Eagle Child lay in wait for him. Eagle Child felt a surge of joy when he identified the dress and saddle markings of the stranger. This was a Piegan Blackfoot!

"Ho, Pikuni!" he called, using the Blackfoot name for his tribe. Eagle Child lifted his arm in greeting. He felt a tingle of happiness at the sound of his own words. It seemed so long since he had greeted a fellow Blackfoot.

The stranger reined in suddenly, holding his rifle at the ready.

"Who are you?" he asked suspiciously. "Are you of the Entrails People?"

Then Eagle Child realized that his oddly assorted clothing would make him hard to identify. Most of it was of Gros Ventre origin.

"I too am Pikuni," he said. "I am Eagle Child, son of Night Rider!"

The other man's face cleared. Night Rider's band was well known because it had once reared a white buffalo calf and had fought a huge raiding party of Assiniboin. But his face clouded again and he stepped back from Eagle Child.

"Last night a rider brought word to our camp that someone in Night Rider's camp has the Spotted Sickness."

Eagle Child's face blanched. "I have been gone from my father's camp since the New Grass Moon. Who has the Sickness? Are many lodges affected?"

The stranger, who identified himself as Little Elk, looked relieved at this. If Eagle Child had not been near the camp, it would be safe to talk with him.

"I heard that only one man has it," he said. "But I don't know this man's name. It is rumored that he caught the Sickness in the land of the Crow. Our man left Night Rider's camp in great fear as soon as he heard about it."

"Where is the camp?" Eagle Child asked. His mind was in a turmoil. If someone had returned with the Sickness it must mean that Sun Boy and Slides-to-the-Ground had arrived home safely. But the fact of the Sickness killed any joy this news might have brought him.

"They are located about one sun's travel beyond where Little River swings toward the Sunrise land," Little Elk told him, "but it would be better if you did not rejoin your people. Perhaps you could return with me to our camp. I could explain that you have not been near the camp of Night Rider. Our people would make you welcome."

Eagle Child shook his head. He would be much less welcome, he thought grimly, when they learned that he too had been in the land of the Crow, and that the infected one had been a member of the same party.

"I must return to my people and share their sorrow. But I will camp apart from them and prepare my own food. Perhaps in some way I can help them."

Little Elk nodded in sympathy. "In time of trouble it is better that a man be near his own people."

"But you have saved me by your warning," Eagle Child said, "and for that you are my brother."

With the coming of darkness, they decided to make camp together. Little Elk tethered his horse in a nearby thicket. All night long the west wind tore at the bushes around them. To Eagle Child — who was restless and awake for much of the time — this was an ill omen. Truly, a summer storm was in the making.

When dawn came, he bade Little Elk good-bye and prepared to head northward. Dark clouds were piling high in the sky. He wanted to get as far as possible before the rain turned the meager prairie streams into raging torrents.

Little Elk watched as Eagle Child trudged off in the distance — a lonely figure in a land robbed of all joy with the absence of sunlight. The older man had toyed with the idea of lending Eagle Child his horse, but it was the best horse he owned. And he did not want any link with a village which had the Spotted Sickness.

Eagle Child reached home in two camps after leaving Little Elk. His progress had been slowed by the heavy rain. Part of Night Rider's village lay in a broad shaft of early-morning sun beside a full-flowing stream which wound back and forth across the shallow valley on its way to Little River. Another section lay on a rise of ground some distance upstream. All of the tipis were farther apart than usual.

For a moment this puzzled Eagle Child, then with

sinking heart, he guessed the reason. They were trying to keep the Sickness from spreading. He sat down on a ridge above the lower group of tipis to think things out. Around him the moist earth steamed with renewed vigor. He could see a tipi with his father's markings in the camp below. Every instinct urged him to rush down there and greet his kinfolk. Coyote was tied by the door, and a brown horse he identified as Red Hawk's. But he could see no sign of Antelope Runner, or his beloved Sun-in-the-Morning. This, too, puzzled him.

A big dog hobbled out from the line of tipis and headed for the silty stream. Eagle Child's heart gave a leap, for he recognized Keewatin, Red Hawk's dog, now grown old and stiff like its master. The young Piegan raised his fingers to his lips to whistle, but he stopped them halfway. If the dog *had* been in contact with the Sickness it would not do to call him.

Which was the infected camp, he wondered? He did not wonder long, for the logic was soon apparent to him. The clean camp would be the one on the higher ground upstream where the earth and water would remain free from all sickness.

As Eagle Child drew near to the upper camp, he was greeted by shouts of welcome from a group of young boys playing beside the nearest tipi. He stopped to ask them who was in this camp when he saw a sight which made him suddenly break into a run. In front of a shabby, unmarked lodge stood Antelope Runner and Sun-in-the-Morning, flicking their tails angrily at the flies that buzzed around them.

At Eagle Child's shout, the red pony threw up its

head and gave a delighted whinny. In a few quick steps, Eagle Child was beside him. He ran his hands caressingly over the sleek coat. The pony nuzzled him fondly. Never again, vowed Eagle Child, would he make a journey without Sun-in-the-Morning under him!

The flap of the tipi was thrown back and Eagle Child's mother stepped out to see the cause of the commotion. Gray Dove stopped in amazement at the sight of her younger son. Her hopes had begun to grow dim, even though Broken Nose and the others had said they found only the body of the mangled horse — that there had been no sign of Eagle Child. And Wolf Calf, the Medicine Man, had backed them up by saying the

spirits always informed him when one of the band went to join the Above Ones.

With a glad cry, Gray Dove embraced him. Eagle Child grinned with happiness. But he grew a little embarrassed as she continued to fuss, for a group of excited children had gathered around them.

"You must be hungry!" his mother said, suddenly recalling the many, many miles he must have traveled.

Inside the tipi she stirred the fire and put on a pot of meat stew which they had had for breakfast.

While she worked, Eagle Child plied her with questions about the disaster which had befallen them.

"Where did you learn of the Sickness?" she asked fearfully. "Did you visit the other camp?"

Eagle Child shook his head. "Two suns ago I camped with Little Elk of Lone Bear's band. He told me a rider had brought word that the Sickness had struck our people."

Gray Dove sighed with relief. Perhaps the Above Ones would be kind and spare this son. If she lost them both she did not know how she would be able to stand it.

Then she told Eagle Child how Slides-to-the-Ground had begun to run a fever the first night that he and Sun Boy arrived home, eight days ago. Two days later the sores had come, then Sun Boy himself was stricken.

"Your father and Wolf Calf ordered that all who had contact with the stricken ones must stay in the lower camp while the rest moved up here. They hope to keep the Sickness from spreading."

"But where is my father, and my brother War Bonnet?" asked Eagle Child, his alarm growing.

"Your brother and his wife are down there," she said sadly. "War Bonnet was one of the first to greet Slides-to-the-Ground and Sun Boy. He wanted to find out if anyone had seen you. Last night he too broke out in a high fever."

"And my father?" Eagle Child said heavily. He felt that he was the one responsible for his brother's trouble.

"Your father is here in this camp. He is holding council with Wolf Calf. Fortunately, when the afflicted ones arrived, more than half of our people were away hunting buffalo," his mother explained. "As we returned at dusk, a warrior came running to say that Sun Boy and Slides-to-the-Ground were back, and that Slides-to-the-Ground was complaining of fever."

"Your father and Wolf Calf thought of the Spotted Sickness at once," she continued. "Broken Nose had told us of the Crow death camp, and how Slides-to-the-Ground had taken a white quiver. They held council with the men of the families which had been hunting. It was decided that all who had not had contact with the Sickness would move their lodges to this camp-site."

"Sun Boy should have known better than to bring Slides-to-the-Ground back!" Eagle Child cried. "It could mean the destruction of our people!"

"He did not know," said Gray Dove. "It is said that Slides-to-the-Ground appeared quite well when they arrived, except that his injured leg was paining.

Sometimes it is many many days before the Spotted Sickness shows itself."

There was a quick step outside and Night Rider came into the tipi. His normally impassive face broke into a broad smile when he saw Eagle Child. No matter what Wolf Calf had said about spirit messages, the Chief believed that no man could survive when his horse was knocked from under him by stampeding buffalo. He had given his younger son up for dead.

Then the smile disappeared as another thought intruded. Night Rider shot a glance at Gray Dove, but she shook her head. "He has not been to the other camp," she said.

"And I was never in that death village of the Crow," Eagle Child assured his father. "It has been more than ten suns since I have seen Slides-to-the-Ground, or Sun Boy."

Night Rider looked relieved. Perhaps, after all, the Above Ones were going to spare him one son.

When Eagle Child had finished eating he sat down for a long talk with his father.

"How is my brother?" he asked.

Night Rider shrugged bitterly. "The medicine of our people is too weak to fight off this White Man's sickness. Your brother is strong of body, but strength alone cannot work miracles."

"Are many stricken?"

"Last night the fever appeared in six lodges. But more are being stricken by the hour. Each morning Wolf Calf and I go to a rise above the other camp. Old Red Hawk comes to the bottom and calls out the names of new victims. Wolf Calf tells him how he can help relieve the pain of the afflicted.''

"If Red Hawk is stricken, who then will carry Wolf Calf's instructions?''

"Old Red Hawk will not get sick. Long ago when the Sickness came to our people he caught it and recovered.''

Eagle Child brightened at this. Sometimes then, the sick ones *did* recover. But, by the look on the faces of his mother and father, his parents did not hold out much hope.

At that moment, the Medicine Man entered. He smiled and nodded at Eagle Child. "Ho, the wanderer returns!'' Wolf Calf had stoutly maintained all along that Night Rider's second son was alive.

"Always the spirits tell me when one of our people has departed,'' he said, looking defiantly at Night Rider.

Night Rider looked uncomfortable. It must be true. Had not his lost son been restored to him?

"Did you get the berries which will ease the sores of the sick ones?'' Gray Dove asked the Medicine Man.

"All the skunkbrush we can find has been picked clean,'' he nodded. "Many women are busy drying and crushing the berries.''

"We will give them the berry powder and we will give them meat, then we must leave,'' Night Rider said firmly.

"Leave?'' Eagle Child asked.

"Two camps to the north of here is a large buffalo herd,'' his father told him. "We will have much need of food, clothing and shelter for the coming winter."

"When the Sickness has run its course, Red Hawk has been told to destroy all the goods of the afflicted ones," the Medicine Man explained.

"But some of our people will surely survive the Sickness?"

"They, too, will burn all their possessions but their weapons and their best set of clothes. When all danger has passed they will rejoin us."

Eagle Child looked at his mother sorrowfully. He knew she had many precious personal things in the other camp that she had been a long time collecting.

But Gray Dove only shrugged. What do goods matter when the lives of her son, daughter-in-law and her good friend Sounding Wind were threatened.

Looking around the tipi, Eagle Child had to admit they would need something better than this for the coming winter. It was made of old lodge covers, torn and patched in many places.

Then his father's voice recalled him.

"You have traveled far, my son. Tell us something of your journey."

Eagle Child told them about the increasing stream of white men through Many Houses, and what the captured Sioux had said about his own land. He described the wagon train at South Bear river and the deep wheel ruts. But when he told of the mighty fireboat, and the big gun it carried, the two older men looked at him in consternation.

"This boat needed no men to paddle it against the full force of Big River?"

Eagle Child shook his head. "The heat from a great fire inside turned a thing called Many Paddles."

They looked at him in utter disblief. "Heat cannot move paddles," Wolf Calf shook his head doubtfully.

"This heat does," Eagle Child told him, "and the big gun shoots bullets the size of a fire stone!"

Wolf Calf and Night Rider exchanged glances. They had heard about the big guns from Indians who had talked with the north traders.

"Perhaps our Head Chief is right," Night Rider grunted. "We will have to learn to accept the white man."

Wolf Calf nodded sadly. "It will not be a good life for us."

Once he had dreamed of becoming a head Sun Priest. Now his own band was even being reduced in size by the Spotted Sickness. And the whole Blackfoot nation was threatened by the growing power of the white man. In what way had they so offended Sun and the other Above Ones?

As Wolf Calf rose to go, Night Rider looked at him inquiringly. "You have consulted the Medicine Pipe bundle?"

The Medicine Man nodded and held up two fingers. "In two suns we will leave for the big hunt," he promised.

After Wolf Calf had departed, Night Rider sat gazing silently into the fire. "Some way must be found to tell our Head Chief of the things you have seen," he said finally.

I 4

♦ ♦
♦

THE WHITE BUFFALO

To the west, the sky was all red and gold as the sun began to slip behind the Backbone. But the beauty of the heavens was lost on Eagle Child. He was tired and hungry. All morning he had slaughtered along the fringes of the retreating buffalo herd. Later, he had skinned each animal, pegging out the hides to dry. His arms ached painfully from his exertions. He knew he had traveled a long way from camp.

"Soon darkness will come," he grumbled to his pony. "Night Light will have to lead us safely home."

The red pony snorted wearily, casting a covetous eye at clumps of succulent bunchgrass as they passed.

Should he cut some meat off one of the carcasses and stop to cook himself a meal, Eagle Child wondered? On second thought, he decided against this. His people would have to come back early — before dawn in fact — to get the meat before many scavengers gathered. Even then, as he well knew, some of the Gray Ones would feast as guests of his hunting prowess. Ordinarily, he would not have killed so many buffalo, but the band was desperately short of hides.

Dusk fell, and Eagle Child swung his pony onto an old buffalo trail which wound up over a long ridge which was studded with poplars. He would save some time this way, he told himself. A slim poplar swayed, but the young rider failed to notice it in the darkness.

Suddenly the silence was shattered by an angry bellow. Both Eagle Child and his pony saw the huge lunging form at the same instant. Wise to the ways of charging buffalo, Sun-in-the-Morning did not need the urgent tug on the reins to wheel sharply away. But the red pony was too late. The great shaggy head with its ugly curved horns caught the horse squarely in the

flank with the force of a battering-ram. Horse and rider went tumbling to the bottom of an open cutbank.

Landing in a clump of bushes, Eagle Child sprang up unhurt. He found his feet in time to see the angry buffalo go thundering off into the dark. The reason he could see the beast so plainly, he suddenly realized, was that the buffalo was white.

Shocked at this betrayal, he stumbled over to where Sun-in-the-Morning lay. He breathed a prayer that his pony had just been knocked unconscious. But in his heart, Eagle child feared the worst. He had seen Sun Boy's horse killed during a hunt in the early spring, so that he was half prepared for what he found.

Sun-in-the-Morning lay dead in a pool of blood. He had died the instant the bull had struck him. Even then, it took several seconds for the full truth to sink in.

The young Piegan let loose a single cry — half of sorrow, half of rage. A hot wave of anger followed, sweeping all other emotions aside. So this was his reward for that day five winters ago when he had found the baby buffalo starving and brought it home to their camp! If only he could have foreseen this moment he would have put an arrow through the white calf's heart!

With the thought of a weapon came a sudden desire to strike back. He would follow the white bull through the darkness like an avenging shadow, and creep up and slay the beast when it stopped to rest. The bull would not travel very far tonight. Somehow he would find it. His hate would be his guide.

Eagle Child felt hurriedly around in the bushes for his bow and quiver of arrows. They had slipped off when he fell. But when he located the bow he soon saw that it was useless, for the binding which held the bow string had torn apart. Frustration piled on anger, and he hurled the bow from him in a rage.

In a little while his anger cooled so that he could think more clearly. He remembered that his father had once warned about decisions made in the heat of anger. They often created more problems than they solved. And hate would make a poor guide. To try to find the bull in the darkness would be an almost hopeless task.

But this bull would surely die, he vowed! He would hunt the betrayer down in a coldly calculated manner which would guarantee success. If he walked the long miles to camp he could rest and refresh himself for the task. At dawn, he would return on his father's swift horse, Antelope Runner, armed with both his bow and his gun.

Eagle Child searched and found the quiver of arrows, then he picked up his discarded bow. Once home, it would take only a moment to slip on a new bow string.

As he turned to leave, his eye fell on the body of his slain pony. Sorrow and compassion welled up in him. Suppose the Gray Ones came to feast as soon as he had gone? As if to confirm these thoughts, a coyote howled out on the grasslands. Did not his boyhood friend Sun-in-the-Morning deserve a far better fate than that?

Eagle Child gently removed his pony's bridle and snare saddle. The cutbank above him suggested a ready solution. Climbing stiffly to the top, he began to push the soft earth and rocks down until the horse was buried deeply enough to ensure that this body would not be disturbed. He finished the job by placing a little pile of stones on the grave so that all would know that a brave and faithful spirit rested here.

Placing the saddle and bridle in the shelter of some bushes, Eagle Child slung the quiver of arrows over one shoulder, took up his bow and set out for home. Soon the moon came up, bathing the rolling plains in a soft glow.

A tipi guard challenged Eagle Child when the latter strode into camp about three hours later. People took turns in staying awake in all the lodges when they were this close to enemy territory. But the man recognized the Chief's son, and went back inside after a word of greeting.

Eagle Child did not want to stop to talk. He headed directly for his father's tipi. Inside, he found both Gray Dove and Night Rider sitting in front of the fire. Apparently neither felt like sleeping.

For a moment he forgot his own troubles in a rush of compassion. It was a desolate place, his father's lodge, without the presence of War Bonnet, his young wife Bright Star, Old Red Hawk and Sounding Wind. Even the big dog, Keewatin, had been a vital part of the family group. He knew that the thoughts of both his parents often dwelt on the stricken camp two days' journey to the south.

Seeing the look on Eagle Child's face, Gray Dove

felt her heart sink. "You have heard word of your brother?"

A month had passed and there had been no sign of any survivors.

Eagle Child shook his head. Her words brought back thoughts of this latest loss he had suffered and his face darkened. Throwing himself down before the fire, he told them what had happened.

"You have traveled far and not eaten," said his mother, rising quickly. Was there no end to the trouble they must suffer, she wondered?

While he ate, Eagle Child outlined his plans for killing the white bull.

"I would like to borrow Antelope Runner," he said, "and range the far hills until I find the bull."

His father looked doubtful. "The White One is no ordinary bull. Perhaps it is even a spirit, as Wolf Calf says. It was decreed by our long ago ancestors that all the White Ones belong to Sun."

"I would make a fine robe from the hide and give it to Sun at the Sun Dance," Eagle Child told him.

"This year, our stricken band will not be welcome at the Sun Dance."

But the Chief was more worried about losing Eagle Child or his favorite horse, Antelope Runner. The bull was said to have killed many men, and often their horses too. It had already killed two horses of Night Rider's band.

"This bull has no fear of a horse and rider," he mused, "and I suppose we are to blame for that. He does not run off in a panic during a chase, but runs with a purpose. Before they know what has happened, experienced riders find themselves and their horses sprawling on the ground."

"Perhaps I could slow the bull down with a gunshot, and then move in and finish him with my bow," Eagle Child suggested. His words ended in a yawn. Suddenly he was tired and ready for his robe. "But kill the bull I must, Father, for he killed Sun-in-the-Morning who was my long-time friend!"

"Often when we kill for vengeance we find we have suffered two losses instead of one," his father said. But he could see that his son was determined about hunting the great bull, so he said no more.

Before rolling up in his sleeping robe, Eagle Child told his parents about the hides and carcasses he had left out on the plains. Night Rider agreed to send butchering parties with the first streak of dawn.

Eagle Child slept fitfully, his dream haunted by glimpses of the good times he had shared with his pony, Sun-in-the-Morning. One scene persisted. He and the pony were frolicking with the white calf. Chasing the belligerent little creature, he would swing the pony in for the pretended kill and send a padded play arrow bouncing off the calf's shoulder. But the white calf soon became wise to the ways of his playmates. As the pony swung in, the calf would suddenly lunge to meet it and Sun-in-the-Morning would grunt at the impact as some of the wind was knocked out of him.

When Eagle Child awoke, the butchering parties were preparing to leave camp. But fragments of his dream remained strongly with him. Springing up, he went to look for his father. He found him talking to some of the scouts who were to make the pre-dawn patrol. Before the Sickness came, this had been Broken Nose's job, the young Piegan thought with a pang.

Night Rider joined him as the scouts rode off. Eagle Child then told his father of the boyhood play scenes he had relived in his dreams. The Chief nodded thoughtfully. This made sense. In spite of what Wolf Calf said, there had to be a practical reason why hunters were unable to close with the white bull.

He had been thinking about Eagle Child's plan to put a single shot into the beast's shoulder and then finish it with the hunting bow, if need be. Night Rider did not like this plan. With one of the new guns which loaded from the back, yes, but a hunter had only one shot with a muzzle-loader.

"Shooting from the back of a bobbing horse you might only nick the bull and anger him," he said. "An angry bull would turn on you. There would be no chance of getting into position for an arrow shot. I would suggest you use my war lance."

Eagle Child's face brightened. Of course — that was it! His father's war lance was six feet long. At intervals on the shaft were wrappings of otter fur so that his hands would not slip. On the business end of the weapon was a twelve-inch metal blade obtained from the north traders. The blade was as sharp as a tip of speargrass.

"I can ride in close enough to guide the blade to its target, but I'll be just out of reach when the bull lunges," he said eagerly.

"If the bull lunges, he will drive the shaft deeper," Night Rider nodded. "Should you fail to hit a vital spot, the shaft will impede him when he tries to turn and charge you."

At noon, Eagle Child set out on the fleet Antelope Runner. In his right hand he carried the war lance. Slung over his shoulder was his repaired hunting bow and a full quiver of arrows. He carried enough dried meat for three days in a small bag which hung from his saddle.

With a final wave of his hand, he swung toward the southeast — the direction the big buffalo herd had been moving when last seen.

Watching him go, Gray Dove knew a mother's misgivings. She was glad Wolf Calf had insisted that her son spend a few hours in a sweat lodge to prepare himself.

"When the young ones grow up they have to follow their own trails," Night Rider consoled her. But he did not feel any happier than she did. There had been too many losses lately for them to bear.

It was early the next morning when Eagle Child sighted the familiar dust clouds rising. Yesterday he had checked three migrant buffalo herds without seeing a sign of his quarry.

Topping a steep rise, he came upon a big herd moving slowly down toward the grassy plains which flanked Little River. Eagle Child turned to the east, setting a course which would bring him in behind the buffalo so that he could ride along without alarming them. There was no sign of the White One.

As they passed between two low cutbanks there was a sudden angry bellow. With a startled snort, Antelope Runner leaped nimbly aside, just in time to miss a furious charge which would have killed him outright. One look at that gleaming white coat told Eagle Child that his search was over.

"Ho!" he screamed defiantly. "You do not do so well when you have to attack in daylight!"

Spinning Antelope Runner around, he followed the plunging bull at a full gallop. The great beast's charge had carried it into the rear guard of the plodding buffalo herd. They scattered and broke into a run. Panic spread quickly through the ranks of their fellows in front, and the whole herd became a bobbing sea of movement. Dust clouds swirled and thickened — adding to the general confusion.

But Eagle Child never once lost sight of his quarry. The fleeing buffalo hampered the white bull's progress. The big beast was unable to push on into the center of the herd, or to turn and menace his pursuers.

Screened by a pair of terror-stricken cows, Antelope Runner steadily narrowed the gap between them. The long legs of the Appaloosa flashed in the morning sunlight. Suddenly the cows veered away, leaving the broad white flank of the bull exposed.

With an exultant yell, Eagle Child swung his horse in for the kill. This was the moment which would test his skill and timing. Raising the long lance over his head with both hands, he sent the weapon hurtling toward that vital spot just behind the bobbing shoulder.

The lance struck just as the white beast lunged side-ways with a savage thrust of its massive shoulder, which would have sent any horse and rider sprawling. But An-telope Runner was a full lance-length away and already swinging out. With a great choking cough the bull top-pled forward, snapping the shaft of the protruding lance when it rolled over and over in a shower of dust.

Around them, the pounding hooves faded as the frightened herd thundered on toward the river.

Eagle Child rode cautiously around the bull. Just to make sure it was safe to move closer, he sent an arrow thudding in beside the broken lance. But he need not have bothered. The lance had penetrated clean to the heart.

As Eagle Child dismounted, his spirits suddenly sagged. It was true, as his father had said. There was no joy in this victory. For as long as the white bull lived, Eagle Child had believed that a great destiny awaited his people — that he himself would play an important role in it.

Now, all he could see ahead was a future as empty as the prairie around him. His father's band was stricken. His brother was dead, and many of his friends with him. No more would he ride out on his pony Sun-in-the-Morning, or see a glimpse of the great white bull among the grazing buffalo. All that remained was the white man with his fireboat and his rolling lodges, each year growing stronger and more numerous.

With a heavy heart, Eagle Child unsheathed his knife and began to remove the white hide. Perhaps next year his band would once more be welcomed at the Sun Dance so that he could offer this hide to Sun.

As he worked, Eagle Child failed to notice the two riders coming across the grassland toward him. His first warning of their approach was a snort from Antelope Runner.

In one stride the young Piegan reached his bow and quiver of arrows. He was fitting an arrow to the bow when one of the approaching men waved an arm and shouted. At the sound of the voice, Antelope Runner threw up his head and whinnied.

Hardly believing his eyes, Eagle Child let the bow and arrow fall. Then he was running to meet his friend Sun Boy and his brother War Bonnet.

"Did the white bull attack you?" Sun Boy asked curiously, after their greetings were over.

"It is true that he did attack," Eagle Child nodded. "But I came seeking to kill."

Then he told them how the bull had killed Sun-in-the-Morning. They walked around the dead beast curiously. War Bonnet removed his father's broken lance from the body and set it on the blood-stained grass.

Eagle Child noted sadly that his brother was thinner and much older-looking and that he walked with a limp. Sun Boy appeared to have stood the Sickness better, although his face was pitted and marked.

"You say the bull attacked in the darkness?" Sun Boy said. "He probably did not know it was you."

Eagle Child looked uneasy. He had not thought of this.

"Are you going to butcher the bull?" War Bonnet asked. He and Sun Boy had traveled far. The idea of a piece of roasted tongue made his mouth water. Like his father, he had never put too much stock in the idea that the bull was a spirit.

Eagle Child shook his head. He pointed toward the grazing Antelope Runner. "There is meat in my saddlebag if you wish to eat."

It did not seem right that they should butcher the white bull.

While the others ate ravenously, Eagle Child continued with the job of removing the hide. As he worked, Sun Boy and War Bonnet told him of the sick camp. Broken Nose had not become sick at all. But Red

Quiver, Woodpecker, Slides-to-the-Ground, Sun Boy's mother and many others had died.

War Bonnet did not mention his wife, Bright Star, or old Sounding Wind. But Eagle Child could tell by his brother's face that these too were lost. Some day he knew War Bonnet would tell them of the long days of suffering in that other camp. He did not care to press him now.

By the time he had finished skinning the bull, Eagle Child had made up his mind what he must do. He pointed to a bank of soft sand some distance away. "We must bury the White One" he said. "We can use our horses and drag the bull over there."

Somehow it did not seem right that the Gray Ones and the scavenger birds should feast on the bull. War Bonnet grunted. He thought this was a lot of unnecessary work, but Sun Boy understood. They stood up to give Eagle Child a hand.

"If I have destroyed a spirit, Sun will surely punish me," Eagle Child said as they pushed the loose sand down on the form of the dead buffalo.

"You can destroy a body but a spirit lives on forever," Sun Boy consoled him. "This morning as we passed a small herd of buffalo your brother pointed to a calf with a white star on its forehead. Is that not so, War Bonnet?"

War Bonnet turned and nodded. He was already climbing up onto his gray pony Coyote, anxious to get home to his people.